Stranger in the House

Stranger in the House

Jane McLoughlin

ROBERT HALE · LONDON

ISBN-10: 0-7090-8159-6
ISBN-13: 978-0-7090-8159-3

Robert Hale Limited
Clerkenwell House
Clerkenwell Green
London EC1R 0HT

2 4 6 8 10 9 7 5 3 1

Typeset in 11½/16pt Palatino
Printed and bound in Great Britain by
Biddles Limited, King's Lynn

one

The train journey from London to Newcastle provided plenty of time for thinking, and I needed to think. My mother had just died and with her my last family tie. It should have been a significant rite of passage for me, face to face with my own mortality. But it wasn't. She seemed like a stranger to me.

I hadn't seen her for years when she died. The last time I came up to Newcastle to see her I sat on the familiar faded old sofa in the front room of the red-brick house while she faced me from my father's battered fireside chair and told me about her only daughter who lived in London. It was a surreal experience, hearing her tell me about myself. I didn't recognize the woman she was talking about. The way she described my life had no connection with the way it felt to me, living it. I felt a detached dislike, in fact, for the daughter she described.

Now my mother was gone and that daughter of hers with her. But everything to do with her death was forcing me back into the past, rolling back the years so that my grown-up self was being consumed by the monstrous child my mother had created. Already, on the train to Newcastle to sort through her things, I was losing touch with the person I thought I was – the successful biographer; the respected academic, awarded the OBE and the American Historical Society's Gold Medal; the widow of a distinguished professor; liver of a comfortable London life full of music, theatre, food and good friends. I felt more like the callow Oxford graduate of my first journey to my parents' new home, where promotion had taken my father. That first journey North had been like travelling to another country. Somewhere near Newcastle, I'd seen a group of ragged women and children scurrying like rats among ravenous gulls on a rubbish tip, and I thought that they looked quaint, picturesque, like photographs from Africa in *National Geographic* magazine, before I realized that these poor scavengers were my own people living life in my own country.

That was then. Now, when we reached Newcastle, the city had lost its alien feel. But I still felt like an intruder as I opened the door to our old house. I'd felt like that when I first came here in 1966, but not in quite the same way. Then I'd been welcomed like the Prodigal Child; and I'd felt guilty because I knew that really I was a cuckoo in the nest.

Now, I had to tell myself that I had a right to be there. Mrs Broderick, my mother's friend, had asked me to come to look through the family papers and take anything I wanted. She'd be away for a week, she'd said. I think she felt embarrassed that my mother had left everything to her and not to me, the blood relation, and wanted to keep out of my way. She needn't have worried. It was only fair. She was the one who was like family to my mother for years, not me.

There were still some of my mother's personal things in the bedroom: grey hairs in the tortoiseshell hairbrush, with matching comb and mirror on the dressing table; the framed photographs of me as a child, posing stiffly in long white socks and over-disciplined hair in thin dark plaits. There were several photos of my parents, always together, always looking like happy lovers. There was a line of books between carved book ends on the chest of drawers. I picked up an old novel by E. Arnot Robertson called *Ordinary Families*. I remembered reading it on that first trip up here, after Oxford, when I was so desperate to escape and start my own life. It had meant a lot to me then. I glanced inside the cover. There was an inscription in my father's writing: 'To my darling Meggie for her birthday from her loving husband Guy, July 1948.' I felt like a voyeur. I'd been four years old then, but I might as well not have existed as part of their marriage.

I wanted to get this over with. Mrs Broderick had left a roll of black plastic sacks. She probably thought I'd want to take most of this stuff back to London. I didn't. I began throwing everything away, clearing first the surfaces of the chest of drawers and dressing table, then what was in the drawers. Mrs Broderick could take all the clothes to Oxfam, I just wanted not to see them. A brown shoe of my mother's distorted by a bunion made me feel ill.

There was a cardboard box at the back of the bottom drawer. I pulled it out and, as I did, the lid fell off and yellowing pieces of paper spilled out. I recognized my own handwriting from long ago. When I started to read, it flooded back. All the hopes and ambitions I'd packed away in that old shoebox I'd forgotten all about. I'd worked hard to forget them. It had taken me months, years.

I spread the pieces of paper over the coverlet. This was all that remained of the book I'd once hoped would bring me fame and fortune. It was to be a biography of Wadhurst Carpenter, the author of *The Seeds of Knowledge*, a man who seemed to me then the antithesis of my stifling, respectable life and my embryonic, timid personality. Wadhurst

Carpenter was my hero: an explorer, a rebel and adventurer, he seemed to me everything real life promised if only I could break out to meet it. Long dead as he was then, killed in North Africa in 1941, he cast a spell over me. I was convinced people would want to read a book about such a man. It would interest publishers. I'd get an advance for research which could take me out of England to Africa and Arabia.

I'd tried to tell Dad about my plan, but of course there was so much I couldn't explain. He thought I should be looking for a husband. It still amazes me that my father, the parent of a daughter who'd graduated from Oxford with a First, could have so little ambition for her, so little awareness of how far her education removed her from his sphere of expectation.

'Why this man Carpenter?' he'd asked. 'Why not someone from round here. What do you know about someone like that, a girl like you?'

And I'd blurted out, 'Don't you see that's the point? Wadhurst Carpenter represents how I want life to be. He's what I want my family to have been; what he did and how he did it is what I wish *our* history had been. If I can do this book about him, I feel I might be able to … I just feel I need to try.' I'd never forgotten the way Dad looked at me then. There was no point in dwelling on it. It was a long time ago.

Back in my mother's old bedroom, the bundle of letters, cards and yellowing, typewritten, foolscap pages scattered across the bed reminded me painfully of the girl I'd been then. I started to sort through them. There was a letter inside an envelope with a London postmark. Wadhurst Carpenter's signature was scrawled at the bottom of a hand-written note on a single sheet of vellum. It read:

My dear old friend,
I was talking to Henriques at the Savoy last night, and
we discussed the deplorable neglect of your early
Arabian paintings, which we agreed are important work
which should be brought to public notice. He suggests
that his firm should sponsor an exhibition which would
tour the major American cities in the summer and
autumn of next year. He is to look further at the feasi-
bility of such a plan, and will contact me before
approaching you directly. I hope I have your agreement
to pursue the matter?

The letter was dated 20 March 1920, and the envelope addressed to Cecil Durrant Esq., Balcurran House, Co. Galway.

The Durrants! Their name still struck a chill of fear down my spine. It seemed incredible, but I hadn't thought of them for years, and at one time I couldn't forget them, or get what happened at Balcurran House out of my head. But Wadhurst Carpenter. I remembered exactly how I'd felt when I first came across this letter to Cecil Durrant in an old file in the Newcastle University library in 1966.

I had permission to do some research there into Wadhurst Carpenter. I'd been lucky. The students were on vacation and the librarian had time to spare. She remembered that a local benefactor who'd made his millions doing deals with the Middle East had left his collection of Wadhurst Carpenter memorabilia to the university. Wadhurst Carpenter had done much of his exploring in Arabia. He had become an impor-tant figure there, the equal of Philby and Lawrence. Maybe there were papers....

She'd brought me the files and I'd found that note to Cecil Durrant. I must have taken it by mistake. I remembered that, at the time, the name Durrant had seemed familiar from footnotes to reference works on Wadhurst Carpenter. I had tried to remember what I knew about Cecil Durrant. To be honest, I hadn't taken much notice. Something about an Englishman who lived out of England, a misfit, a devout but eccentric Christian who, as a young man, travelled as a pilgrim alone and almost penniless among the Moslems in the deserts of Arabia, late in the nineteenth century; a painter and geologist whose illustrated notebooks had provided Carpenter with a crucial guide in his own later journeys in the desolate Nejd region.

I had turned over the sheet of paper and on the back was a sketch drawn in fading inks. It showed an old, bent man leaning on a stick. A few straggling lines of bright red ink grew out of his chin and above his ears. A tiny, stiff-backed woman with a pile of luxuriant black-ink hair high on her head stood at his side. The couple were flanked by two tall, gawky girls, with identical short, straight hair cuts and shapeless flowered dresses. They'd looked to me like naively-carved gateposts framing the bent man and the tiny woman. A caption under the sketch read: 'Family Blessings', then, added in darker ink, 'My blessings on you, with Nasramy's grateful thanks'. And 'Balcurran House, 1932'.

That was Cecil Durrant's reply to Wadhurst Carpenter's note. Even now I remembered how I felt all those years ago when I first saw that sketch. I had stared at the picture of the old man, who had apparently meant so much to my hero, with his wife and daughters. It was the unthinking sketch of a considerable artist, demonstrating his skill even though it was merely something dashed off to amuse. The old man looked as though he was on the point of death, so frail he might have blown away in a puff of wind. He could have been posing for a portrait of King Lear. His wife, in contrast, stood as straight and firm as a toy soldier on sentry duty. She was much, much younger than her husband. The daughters might have been any age at all, overgrown schoolgirls even, with slides holding back their bobbed hair and funny, flat-heeled, buttoned shoes.

At the time I wondered how that old man had married a woman so much younger than himself? Could she really be the mother of those strong, lanky girls, both big and bony, though one was thin and the other more heavily built? They towered over her, and over the feeble old man leaning on his stick. I was young and immature, but even then there was, to my mind, something odd about those young women, as if they'd become adults without ever reaching puberty. Or perhaps it was the artist's attitude that was odd, that he saw them as perpetual children.

Their mother was different, though. Defiant, she stood there denying time and gravity, seeming to be holding the world at bay so that the old, old man would be protected from knowing how completely he had been forgotten.

I'd gone back to the librarian and said I needed to find out what I could about a painter called Cecil Durrant. There wasn't much. Born 1856, married in 1894, in Italy, to Caroline Willoughby-Ingram, twenty-year-old third daughter of General Sir Montague Willoughby-Ingram. Their two daughters, Patience and Hilda, were born in 1902 and 1904.

It was 1966. Those girls could still be alive. And if they were, the Durrant daughters could help me. They might well remember Wadhurst Carpenter. They'd have met him, known him as a family friend, heard him talk about his work with their father. They might have letters and mementoes which would shed new light on the great man.

The librarian had been sifting through a reference book. 'There's something here about a Patience Durrant,' she said. 'According to this, she was quite a distinguished scientist, some sort of botanist. One of the daughters?'

I was surprised. I knew very little then about anything scientific. I think I'd taken it for granted that a skill as technical as botany would be an exclusively masculine world for someone of Patience Durrant's age. I asked the librarian if there was any mention of the other sister. I tried to make a joke. 'Don't tell me, she's a brain surgeon?'

Hilda Durrant, it seemed, was also well-known in her day as a painter of flowers and plants.

From that moment, I'd had a weird feeling about the Durrants. Indeed still, all these years later, this sudden reconnection with them gave me a reminder of some of the excitement of discovery I felt then.

two

There were several sheets of foolscap stuck in the shoebox among the letters and notes. They were covered in bad typing on a machine which needed a new ribbon. I remembered now. I'd made a start on a book, but it wasn't the Wadhurst Carpenter book I'd planned. I gave it a scientific-sounding title, *Making Man Of A Myth: Nature v Nurture*. I suppose I'd intended to set the scene for Wadhurst Carpenter, but it reads now like a historical romance, and it doesn't seem as bad to me as it did when I wrote it:

From a sun-drenched villa on the slopes of Alassio, in the autumn of 1894, the three young daughters of General Sir Montague Willoughby-Ingram watched the daily train of donkeys struggling up the hillside to the Villa Previ, laden with panniers of fruit, meat and bread; and they speculated upon the appetite of the hungry *Inglese* who lived there.

Constance, the eldest, was the only one who had ever seen him. 'He's enormously tall and covered in reddish hair and he wears funny little spectacles like an old man in a story by Mr Dickens,' she told her sisters.

'He sounds to me more like Dr Jekyll and Mr Hyde,'

Helen said. 'Wasn't Mr Hyde covered in red hair? And the hungry *Inglese* never goes out except at night. He spends all day painting huge pieces of canvas in different shades of yellow.' She sensed that her sisters did not believe her. 'That's what Guiseppe told Mother's maid,' she said. Then she said 'Oh, damn,' and began to suck the finger she had pricked on her embroidery needle.

Caroline, the youngest sister, yawned. 'Well of course he spends all his time painting,' she said with scorn, 'he's a painter. He probably has an exhibition coming up. I heard Papa say that he has quite a reputation among people who know about these things.'

'That doesn't make him a good painter,' Helen said. 'The reputation might be for anything. He could be a Casanova.' She giggled as Constance looked shocked. 'Anyway,' she added, 'he can't really be well-known or he wouldn't be so poor.'

'He can't be so very poor when he eats as much as he does,' Caroline said. Her dark eyes followed the flicking tail of the last of the donkeys as it disappeared up the steep track.

'His servants are cheating him,' Constance said. 'An old man on his own would never notice that the staff are ordering extra and stealing his food.'

'But that is shocking,' Caroline said. 'I'll tell Mother. She'll know what to do.'

There was a short silence. A salamander ran across the baking stone terrace in front of a one-eared tabby cat stretched along the balustrade, in the shade of an over-hanging mimosa. The cat opened an eye and flexed its claws.

'Is he old?' Caroline asked.

'Is who old?' Constance was almost asleep.

'The hungry *Inglese*.'

'He looks old,' Constance said, 'almost as old as Papa. As old as Mother, anyway.'

'I don't care how old he is,' Helen said. She laid aside her sewing. 'It would be nice to see a new face so late in the season. I hope Mother calls on him. We should tell her she should. At least he must speak English. He can marry Constance and live happily ever after.'

Constance, facing her twenty-sixth birthday in a few weeks, was hurt. She was becoming conscious that she had not yet had a proposal of marriage, and there seemed fewer eligible young men than ever in Alassio this season. To make it worse, Papa and Mother seemed little interested in meeting the people who were still there. But Caroline, who at just twenty had very little understanding of her sister's feelings, laughed at Helen's idea.

'If he is a painter,' she said, 'he probably drinks too much and leads a dissolute life with his models. He'll create a career out of painting Constance in the nude and make her famous for her harmonious mass.'

'Well, I hope he gets over his passion for yellow,' Constance said, refusing to be drawn. It was too hot.

Caroline heard the note of irritation in her sister's voice. She was not inclined to tease her further. It was far too sultry to have to put up with one of Con's sulks.

'We'd see the bottles,' she said. 'If he drank, we'd see the bottles in the panniers.'

'Actually, he can't be a Casanova either,' Helen said. 'He's practically a priest, he's so Christian. Or so Guiseppe told Maria.'

'You mean he's a Catholic?' Caroline asked.

'Oh, no, he's as Anglican as we are, but sort of dedicated.'

'He doesn't come to our services,' Constance said.

'Apparently someone said that to him, and he said "I am always in church",' replied Helen.

'According to Guiseppe,' Caroline said.

There was nothing more to say. The three young women lay on the terrace under the awning. The wind scarcely stirred the leaves of the olive trees which overhung the path leading down to the village. The air was heavy with the scent of bougainvillea.

Soon Constance and Helen slept. Caroline got up and walked to the edge of the terrace, leaning over the balustrade to look across at the shimmering bronze haze of the sea beyond the olive grove. Beyond that was Africa, where the sun burned an even fiercer orange and the heat pounded people's brains and turned the earth to powder. She didn't know if that was true, but it was how she imagined it. I wonder what it's really like? she asked herself. When am I going to be able to find out such things for myself? And she thought of the hungry *Inglese* covering his canvas with hot yellow paint. He must know what it was like out there beyond the sea. Papa had told them that their mystery neighbour was an explorer who disappeared for months at a time, years even, wandering among alien people in lands where no Englishman had lived before, collecting notes and sketches for his pictures.

She caught a movement on the rocky track. She shielded her eyes against the glare and saw a skeletal silhouette against the rock.

'It is he,' she said under her breath, 'it's the hungry *Inglese*.'

She hurried through the house to reach the door before he could knock and wake the others. When she appeared at the top of the steps, the visitor stopped and stared at her.

'Come in,' Caroline said. Inexplicably, she was finding it difficult to draw enough breath to speak to him. 'Everyone's asleep, but they won't be long.'

Constance had been right, he did give an impression of redness – red beard, red hair under his straw hat, reddish freckles thick on his sun-reddened face. But he was nothing like Mr Hyde. Caroline saw him more like the flame of a candle. He had quite the wrong colouring for wandering in the desert, even if he shrouded himself in the long robes the Arabs wore. She thought he looked as though he needed someone to look after him.

'I'm Caroline Willoughby-Ingram,' she said, 'and you are the hungry *Inglese* from the Villa Previ.' In the two o'clock silence of the sleeping afternoon, she felt the trite words were tossed far and wide across the rocky hillside in mockery. She flushed, feeling childish under the gaze of his fierce green eyes.

He bowed to her. 'Indeed, I come to visit General Willoughby-Ingram. I wish to consult him on a question of the geography of Rome. I believe he knows that city well.' There was a curious archaic cadence to his speech. He spoke slowly as though he was so unused to company that he had to limber up even in his own language.

'That is indeed so,' Caroline said, realizing that she was echoing his old-fashioned speech pattern. 'He will be here directly,' she said in a more normal voice.

She led him into the drawing-room. She wanted to keep him away from her sisters; she wanted to keep him to herself and watch him undisturbed as though he were some exotic captive bird. An injured bird, she thought, I wish he were a bird and I would cure and care for him so that he can fly free again. To calm him, distract him from trying to escape, she tried to make conversation.

'We watch the donkeys taking the supplies up to your villa every day,' she said. 'We are amazed how much you eat.' The blinds were lowered at the windows against the sun. It was dim and cool in the room. Caroline could not see his face clearly.

'I thought you would be an enormous fat man,' she said. She knew she was being foolish and insulting but she didn't seem able to stop herself.

'I eat sparsely. The servants are probably taking the food,' he said. He did not seem indignant.

'But that is terrible,' Caroline cried. 'You can't let them get away with that.'

He smiled at her. 'I have no doubt that they have need of it,' he said. 'I do not begrudge them.'

'Then you should,' she said. 'If one of us lets them get away with it, they'll expect more from the rest of us.'

'So young, and yet already the instincts of the English household matron are so strong in you,' he said. He sounded full of regret.

Caroline wanted to feel angry, but in fact she was afraid she might burst into tears. She felt as though she had been unconscious and he had suddenly slapped her on the face and brought her out of a long coma. It was the first time she had ever felt that her familiar way of life was a stilted, stultifying thing that she could not defend.

'I'm sorry,' she said, faltering, 'I think I hear my father coming now.'

He started to say something, but she was running out of the room. She passed her father on the stairs.

'How can you run like that in this heat?' he asked, grumbling.

'I was coming to look for you,' she said. 'You have a visitor.'

She ran on up the stairs and locked the door of her bedroom behind her. She was overwhelmed by the certainty that nothing in her life would ever be the same again. But that's absurd, she told herself, of course it will. It has always been the same, it always will be. But she knew it *was* changed, because she would never be wholly content with it again. She wanted to talk to someone, to tell someone, but tell them what? Nothing had happened. Nothing had changed except herself. She must pull herself together and stop being so silly. Mother's reaction would be to give her a dose of salts and a talking to, but this was something she couldn't try to explain even to Mother. She thought, I'm not a child any more, in a moment, just like that, I'll never be a child again.

A sudden breeze moved the blinds at the windows. Outside someone shouted at the back of the house where the servants lived, a woman laughed. Caroline heard her mother's footsteps on the stairs. She was calling for Constance, looking for her daughters. The siesta was over.

Caroline looked at herself in the mirror. She looked exactly the same as she had that morning when she got up; exactly the same as before lunch or an hour ago when she had come upstairs for her book to read on the terrace.

She smoothed her dark hair and held a handkerchief soaked in eau de Cologne against her hot forehead. She ran downstairs after her mother.

Her father was standing in the hall. She slowed to a walk for the last few stairs. He was frowning, his hand stroking his chin. He was staring at her, but there was a puzzled look in his eyes, as though he was not sure who she was.

'Good afternoon, Father,' she said, standing on tiptoe to kiss his cheek. 'Has your visitor gone already?'

He started, then said, 'You met Mr Durrant, then?'

'The hungry *Inglese*? Is he Mr Durrant? He didn't tell me his name. He said he wanted to ask you about Rome. I was sure you could help him.'

'Ask me about Rome? What about Rome?'

'He said he had a question of geography he hoped you might be able to answer.'

'Oh, he had a question for me, indeed he did,' General Willoughby-Ingram said in the sort of tone he reserved for telling army stories with his old soldier friends.

Caroline started to move away.

'Don't you want to know what he asked me?' her father said.

'He *said* it was about Rome,' Caroline said.

'He wanted to ask permission to marry you,' her father said. It was as if he needed to say it aloud before he could express his astonishment. The words helped make the fact real. But he couldn't believe what he was saying.

'Oh,' Caroline said in a whisper.

Her father looked at her as though he was expecting her to laugh. 'He doesn't even tell you his name and he wants to marry you, what do you make of that?' he said. She could tell from his tone that here was the makings of a first-class story over the port.

'I think yes,' she said, 'yes, I will be very happy to marry him.'

three

That was as far as I got with the book. But I didn't give up on the Durrants. The reply to the letter I must have written to the daughters at the address in Co. Galway, where Wadhurst Carpenter had sent his letter to their father, was among the relics in the shoebox on my mother's bed. I don't remember exactly what I wrote to them, but here was their reply.

Dear Miss Weaver,

My sister and I have carefully considered your letter. We note that you intend to write a book about our father's former protégé, Wadhurst Carpenter, the author of The Seeds of Knowledge. *We have been approached from time to time over the years by authors seeking information on Wadhurst Carpenter, who was, as you state, a frequent visitor to our home here in the years before our father died in 1935. However we have invariably turned down such requests, which we have always felt would involve an unwarranted intrusion on our privacy.*

However, in your letter, you express a real interest in our father Cecil Durrant's own life and contribution to Wadhurst Carpenter's work and reputation. You imply that you feel previous biographers have failed to give due recognition to the importance of Cecil Durrant in making Wadhurst Carpenter's achievements possible. We share this view. If you have a genuine concern to redress this balance and to give our father the acknowledgement he deserved, we will be glad to welcome you to Balcurran House. There are a considerable number of letters and notebooks which passed between the two of them, and in principle we are willing to allow you access to these. I do not know what there is which might interest you, since our father's papers have been left untouched since he died. But I know he made copies of all his important letters.

My sister Patience and I will be happy to give you what information we can about our father's life and work, but there is little we can tell you about Wadhurst Carpenter. Though he visited our family home frequently, our contact with him was restricted to brief encounters at meals, and neither our father nor Wadhurst Carpenter were men prepared to discuss their work or views on serious issues while we were present.

Balcurran House itself may help you to gain an impression of our father and his attitude to his work. The defining theme of his work and his life was his love of his own country, in which, of course, as a man of his own time, he included Ireland. He settled here when he ceased to travel and came back to his homeland to create finished paintings from the sketches he made on his foreign journeys. Both my sister and I were born in Italy, though we do not remember living anywhere but Balcurran House. Our parents were concerned to find somewhere where my father could work without distraction, in total solitude except for his family. Our home also had to be big enough that we children could not disrupt him while he worked.

We were a close and very happy family, and, as a family, we always kept his working time sacrosanct – a habit of discipline my sister and I still retain between ourselves.

To continue, my parents had almost given up hope of finding the right place when they heard through friends about this isolated house on the Galway coast overlooking the sea. An elderly couple had built the house and lived there for some years. They had recently died, and no one had been there since. My parents had to walk five miles from the nearest village to find the place, but when they did, my mother refused to leave. My father had to abandon her there and walk back alone to make all the arrangements. My sister and I have lived at Balcurran House ever since. We stayed on with our mother after our father died, and then together after she was sadly taken from us after the 1939–45 War.

If you will let us know when you are coming, we can put you up at Balcurran House. We have plenty of room here. Also, the house is in an isolated position, and there is nowhere conveniently close where you could stay while you study our father's papers. I expect to hear from you.

Yours sincerely, Hilda Durrant.

Ireland had come as a shock to me, I know that. It seemed so much the same as England and at the same time so different. As a teenager I'd gone on a school trip to Paris, and then I'd expected the foreignness of France, except in those days I didn't think of it as foreign, more like something laid on to entertain us English, unreal, like a stage set. Ireland looked so much the same as home, but in so many little things, from the name of the port, Dun Laoghaire, to the Gaelic script on the public lavatories and the green telephone boxes, it seemed to me too deliberately different from Newcastle, let alone Oxford or Woking, to be unreal. For the first time in my life, I felt I was not at home. The sound of English being spoken, the smell of the harbour, the horses pulling rattling carts among the cars on the streets – all seemed familiar, but like a memory from a previous life. It seemed to me that, here, it was I who was unreal.

An ancient bus waited at the dockside. With other dazed and fumbling English passengers from the boat, I climbed on board and we waited in anxious silence until all the seats were filled. Then a driver in a ramshackle uniform suddenly appeared and we were rumbling through part-familiar, part-alien streets, and I didn't care whether this was the bus to Dublin or not because there was nothing I could do about it. I felt like Alice in Wonderland, a feeling which stayed with me throughout the endless train journey into the night towards the west coast. Travelling in the dark always seems to slow the clock and the trip seemed interminable. It felt like hours before we stopped in Athlone, then hours more before we set off again at last.

Until the moment we left the street lamps of the Athlone suburbs behind, it had been easy for me to tell myself that nothing had happened. There'd been no sense of the enormity of what I was doing. I was on my way to Balcurran House; I had told my parents I was going, I'd signed the papers for an overdraft at the bank, and I'd gone, and now I was in Ireland, and none of it seemed real.

Then, later still, on a rainswept platform at Athenry, in a pool of yellowish light so dim that I wondered if the Irish still had gaslights, my hands blistered by the handle of my suitcase, I watched the dark shape of the train disappear down the line. A sudden red light filled the black gap it left. I looked across the platform for some sign of life. A door slammed in a huddle of distant buildings. There was a light shining behind a fogged-up window. Someone shouted in what sounded like a foreign language. It hadn't occurred to me that my journey could come to a full stop long before I reached my destination. I had written to Hilda Durrant to say the day and time when I was starting the journey, but after that I thought that the travelling would be a simple question of catching boats and trains. In fact, I hadn't given it a thought. In my mind it was the going which was the giant step; the rest was a distraction. The worst that could happen would be having to wait for connections. Then, when I arrived as close as I could get to Balcurran House, I assumed I would telephone the house and Hilda Durrant would send someone in a car to meet me. It couldn't be far, for had not Hilda herself mentioned that the nearest village was only five miles away from the house? And she had been talking about many years ago when her parents first saw the place. The village now was probably a full-blown seaside resort which had developed to within easy reach of Balcurran House.

I dragged the suitcase along the platform towards the lit window. A woman with nicotine-stained fingers and dirty nails was sitting on one of several upright wooden chairs, reading a newspaper beside a reluctant fire in a small black grate. I knocked on the window. The woman looked up. She folded her newspaper and laid it on the chair before coming slowly to the window and peering out at me. I made a gesture asking her to open the window to speak to me. She shook her head and seemed about to pull down a blind.

'Wait,' I said, 'I only want information.'

'Booking office is closed,' the woman said. She seemed

almost afraid of me, the way she looked me up and down, staring at my clothes. I'd never thought of myself as fashionable, but perhaps even my standard 1960s miniskirt and stiletto heels were outlandish in this place.

The woman's voice was faint through the glass although her mouth worked and she seemed to be trying to pronounce the words clearly for me to understand. 'You'll have to come back in the morning,' she said, sounding as though she was trying to communicate with a monkey in a zoo.

'I'm trying to get to Balcurran House,' I said. 'Can you help me?'

'Balcurran House?' It sounded quite different the way she said it. 'You won't get there from here, not tonight you won't. Nor any other time by train.' She laughed, but I didn't see the joke.

At last she pulled up the sash and opened the window a few inches. 'God help you now, the only way you'll reach anywhere tonight is to find a taxi to take you there,' she said. 'And taking a taxi from here to anywhere at all, let alone Balcurran House, would cost you more than a decent man could earn in a month round these parts.'

'Do they take cheques?' I asked.

'No credit,' the woman said. She was definitely suspicious of me now. She shut the window with a bang and mouthed at me from behind the glass again. 'You might get a ride in the cattle lorry as far as Oughterard.'

'Is that near Balcurran House?' I asked, pressing my face against the glass so she would hear.

She shook her head. 'I wouldn't say near,' she said.

'But I could get to Balcurran from there?'

'Sure you could indeed.'

'Easier than from here?'

'I wouldn't like to say that,' she said, 'that's hard to say.'

'So why go there?'

'That's not for me to say, it's you is making the journey.'

'But I want to go to Balcurran.'

'Sure, didn't I hear you say so, and didn't I tell you you can't get there from here, not tonight?'

'But why did you suggest this Oughterard?'

'Because that's somewhere you can go. I was trying to be helpful.' It was clear she wanted to be rid of me.

'But there's no way of getting to Balcurran from here?'

She seemed to consider this. 'Mick Power has a car. He might take you,' she said at last.

'Where'll I find him, this Mr Power?' I was shouting, mouthing at her too as though she were the animal in the zoo.

'Wouldn't you find him in the bar across the way,' she said. 'And if he isn't there he won't be anywhere else, I'm thinking.' She pointed fiercely to her right.

Mick Power was indeed in a bar opposite the entrance to the station. At first he was unwilling to take me. But trade had been bad that day and in the end he was prepared to make a deal. It took all the cash I'd brought with me, but I told myself that I could cash travellers' cheques next day.

'Do you know where we're going?' I asked him.

'Sure we'll know it when we get there,' he said.

There was nothing more I could say.

Once we had left Athenry and were speeding into the dark void, he turned on a small transistor radio that dangled on a string from the driving mirror, and beat time to the music with his fingers on the wheel.

'Isn't it Brendan Boyer who's the greatest singer in the world today?' Mick Power said.

Something stopped me saying that I'd never heard of Brendan Boyer but that to my mind he was no Elvis, and Mick seemed satisfied at my silence. I wished that he would turn it off, but I kept quiet, at least I didn't have to make conversation. I tried to ignore the persistent drumbeat pulsing in my head, but gradually it seemed to become an expression of my growing frustration with the driver and the endless journey and I was glad of it.

Perhaps Mick Power was lost. I would never know. Twice he stopped in the middle of nowhere saying he was going to ask a man he knew the way to go from there. The first time I thought he needed to answer a call of nature, but then there was a flash of light as he opened a door and a sudden burst of raised voices before he disappeared and the darkness settled round me once more. When he returned the first time, he said cheerfully, 'Well, not far to go now,' and whirled me off into the unknown.

The second time he got into the driving seat and turned to face me. 'Are you certain sure in your mind you want to go to this Balcurran?' he asked.

'Yes,' I said.

He shrugged and started the engine. I heard him mutter, 'Don't be saying afterwards you weren't warned.' He set off as though he was taking some kind of revenge on me for being an awkward passenger.

At last he turned off the road and stopped. The arc of the car lights revealed towering wrought iron gates between vast stone posts. Beside the right post was a narrow wooden stile.

'This is the place,' he said. He pointed at a peeling painted board fixed to the gate post: BALCURRAN HOUSE ONLY. TRESPASSERS WILL BE PROSECUTED.

I could see no sign of habitation, no lights, no shadowy

shapes of buildings. 'But this is only the end of a drive,' I said. 'This isn't a house.'

The driver got out of the car and walked across to the gates. There was a heavy chain holding the gates closed. He gave this a token rattle, standing back so that I could see the padlock.

'This is as far as I can go,' he said. He opened the rear door of the car. I was afraid he was going to pull me out.

'But it could be miles yet,' I said. 'What about my suitcase?'

'I think I saw a light through the trees,' he said. 'I'm sure it's not far. I'll help you put the case over the fence and you can leave it to be picked up later if it's too heavy.'

'But you can't simply leave me here like this. Look at my shoes.' I was pleading with him.

'I can't take you any further, and you won't deny that this is the place you wanted to come.' Then he seemed to relent. 'What I can do is take you to the nearest place on my way home and drop you there.'

I hesitated. I had no cash left, and no hope that my cheque book would be of use out here. I couldn't afford to stay a night in a hotel.

'Make up your mind, me darlin',' he said, 'this is no place to pass the time on a dark night with a long drive before me to get home to my wife and children, not to mention the wife's mother, bad cess to her.' He went to lift the suitcase out of the back of the car and in the courtesy light I saw him look at me for my decision.

The gates and the trees behind them looked spectral in the car lights. I very nearly told him that he could take me back to Athenry with him. I would take the next possible train back to Dublin and be back in Newcastle by this time tomorrow. But then I thought of the look Dad and Mum would give each other when I walked into the house, the little gloat of a smile they'd have because that was the end of all my nonsense about a career and being independent.

Mick Power seemed to be having second thoughts about leaving me. At least he waited long enough for me to climb the fence in the light of his headlights. Then he drove off.

The sudden silence was scary, and the darkness was like a hood over my face. I stood and listened. Then I became aware of all sorts of sounds – small rustlings in the bushes on either side of me, the snap of a twig, the faint muffled twitterings of sleepy birds disturbed. My eyes gradually began to grow accustomed to the darkness, and in fact it probably wasn't a particularly dark night. Only a thin cover of cloud hid a bright full moon and at intervals this cast a shadowy light over the track ahead, reflecting off the surface of great puddles in the driveway.

If Mick Power hadn't been lying when he said he'd seen a light from the house, I could see no sign of it now. I struggled forward, half dragging, half carrying, the suitcase. Several times I tripped over unseen obstacles in the road, and once I caught my foot in one of the brambles creeping unchecked across the path. I nearly fell and felt a sharp pain as the briar tore my ankle. My feet were soaking wet and cold where I'd walked into puddles, and there was a small sucking sound of mud when I clenched and unclenched my toes inside my shoes.

The dark mass of a house loomed suddenly ahead. I had an impression of vast bulk. A sudden snatch of moonlight revealed steps to a pillared porch. Bright cloud reflecting off a battery of windows, like bespectacled eyes, gave me the feeling that I was being watched from behind a curtain.

I climbed bone-white moonlit steps to the front door. There was an old-fashioned metal bell-pull, dark against pale stone, beside the door. I jerked it and heard a hollow clang echo inside the house.

Nothing happened. I stepped back down the steps and peered up to see if a light came on at one of the windows, but there was no sign of life. I tugged at the bell-pull again and heard a tolling which should've been enough to waken the dead. I banged on the door with my fists.

The door was suddenly dragged open onto a dimly-lit hallway. Someone said roughly, 'Come in if you're coming.' I picked up my case and stepped inside. The door was slammed heavily behind me.

I found myself staring at a young woman wrapped in a plaid blanket. Her pale face was almost hidden behind a tangle of wild reddish hair. The hand that clutched the rough wool across her breasts was covered in freckles. The young woman pushed back her hair with her free hand, revealing one side of her face. I found myself looking into a greenish, pale-rimmed eye that had no expression.

'I'm Frances Weaver,' I said, 'Miss Durrant is expecting me.' I started to babble, trying to explain my sudden appearance in the dark.

The young woman stared at me. She turned and padded away, disappearing at once into the shadows. I waited, wondering what to do. I moved further into the room and looked about me.

Inside the door there was a model of a three-masted sailing ship standing on a wooden chest. The vessel seemed to be built to scale, about five feet long and seven or eight feet to the top of the main mast. At the prow, a sightless painted mermaid figurehead pointed the way forward.

Apart from the model ship, there was no furniture in the hall. There were closed doors on either side which must have led to other rooms. Shallow stone steps opposite the main door led up to a landing at the far end of which I could see a huge stained glass window. A wide wooden staircase rose off the landing.

I waited. I did not know what else to do. I felt cold, chilled by all the stone and the churchy atmosphere. The house had an odour of its own, as though the air in the place was very old and tainted by damp dust and the breath of dead generations. I looked for a chair but there was none, so I sat as best I could on my suitcase. I was exhausted and miserable, afraid that I would burst into tears. But there was something about the wintry atmosphere of the house which made me afraid to open the doors to those other rooms. The place felt unfriendly, as though wanting me to leave. I wished I'd gone back to Athenry while I'd had the chance.

Then there was the sound of a door closing and quick footsteps on the stairs. I looked up. In the gloomy light I saw a huge angular figure rushing down towards me, a spectral shadow against the white wall, like an illustration of a wicked witch in a child's book of fairy tales. The grotesque figure reached the foot of the stairs and became a mere woman, no witch but an elderly schoolmarmish woman with grey hair and soft pink-and-white skin. She was tall and thin, her grey hair cut short in the same straight bob held back by a slide that I remembered from the sketch on Cecil Durrant's card to Wadhurst Carpenter. I would have known her anywhere, though in his drawing her father had shortened the long, curved, cartoon-character nose. I supposed that to copy that hawk-like beak to the life would have turned his sketch into a caricature.

This was Hilda Durrant. She was dressed in a dark straight tweed skirt, high-necked grey blouse and long grey cardigan. The faint squeak of her flat-heeled shoes on the flagstones put my teeth on edge. She emitted a musical scale of little cries as she approached me in a series of scuttling darts, like some huge mouse.

'You poor little thing,' she said, 'we were sure you couldn't get here before tomorrow and now you're here and have taken us by surprise. You must be tired out. Are you hungry? Come to the kitchen and we'll find something for you to eat. What about tea? Or coffee?'

I had to crane my neck to look up at Hilda Durrant's face. I thought she must be nearly six feet tall, though she'd obviously got into the habit of stooping. When she was still, she stood like a perched vulture. This Hilda was a scrawny bird of prey, and I myself felt like a small rodent about to be pinned down by that long curved beak. But when she moved I saw that I was being ridiculous, there was nothing threatening about this funny old woman; she was no bird of prey, more like a moth-eaten old hen with a chick.

A clock struck the hour. I lost count of the strokes.

'I'm afraid I've got you out of bed, it must be so late,' I said. God, what made me say that? Hilda had obviously got dressed deliberately so I wouldn't think that.

'Oh, no,' Hilda said, 'I hadn't retired. I'm not a good sleeper. I often read into the early hours.'

'I am tired,' I said, 'really all I want is to go to bed.'

Hilda did not argue and picked up the suitcase with such ease that I did not protest that I could carry it myself. I followed her, trying to keep up as she strode upstairs and along a dark narrow passage.

'This is your room,' came her voice from the shadows. She

opened a door and turned on a light. I saw curtains in a fussy, flowered material, a narrow brass bed, and the reflection of Hilda's bird-like profile in a large gilt mirror over a dressing table opposite the bed. 'The bathroom's next door,' she said. 'I'm afraid there won't be enough hot water for a bath until morning. Breakfast is at eight. I hope you'll be comfortable. Sleep well.' Then she was gone.

four

Left alone in that bedroom at Balcurran House I felt like a new girl at school. The bedroom had the same slightly disinfectant smell. But at school I'd had the company of Alison Tate, and now for the first time in years I found myself thinking of her, and, frankly, wishing she were here with me.

Alison was the nearest I'd ever come to having a best friend. We'd been in the sixth form together. Our school was a girls-only establishment in Surrey, where we were being educated to become nice middle class wives and mothers to men just like our fathers. Alison and I were the odd ones out because we didn't want that. Actually we had very little else in common. I was studious and bent on getting to Oxford to study history; she was horse-mad, seeing books and homework as part of a conspiracy to stop her becoming the first woman to ride in the Grand National. Some hope, poor Alison. During the holidays she worked as a stable girl in the local riding school. But we were friends because there was no one else.

For much the same reasons we kept in touch for a while after we left school. I went up to Oxford where everyone seemed so much more sophisticated, glamorous and self-confident than I did, and I found it hard to make new friends.

Alison went to work for a racehorse trainer as a stable girl, but she was still too ambitious to become a jockey herself to be able happily to make do with sex and riding out like the other girls. We were both lonely and we wrote long angst-filled letters to each other. She had a great love of Gothic novels, and replying to her letters gave me the chance to dramatize myself in a way I could never dare in everyday life. Even so, our correspondence had gradually dwindled.

Recently, though, I'd heard she'd broken her leg in a fall, and it seemed to me that writing to her now would make me feel closer to her again. I needed someone to talk to, and Balcurran House was a perfect setting for stories of Gothic imagination to pass her idle hours. Besides, what was happening to me now was making me painfully aware that I was very much on my own, and I needed someone to tell my innermost thoughts. Alison was the only person I could think of who fitted the bill. So, on my first night at Balcurran House, I wrote to her.

Dear Alison,

This is just a note to tell you that I've arrived at this place to do some literary research on a man I hope to write a book about. Don't ask me why I'm sitting up in bed in the coldest room I've ever been in, writing to you. I'm expecting a headless ghost to start walking any minute. It's just so that if I disappear suddenly off the face of the earth, you know where to start looking. Mind you, I can't tell you where the hell I am, it seems to be a million miles from nowhere in Ireland, which is definitely, judging by my experience so far, Cloud Cuckoo Land.

That's it, so far. But I'll keep you in the picture. I can't explain why this place is so spooky, but think of Count

Dracula's castle and Red Riding Hood's granny and you'll have some idea. Were there mice at Castle Dracula? There are here, or else the place really is haunted. I'm sure everything will seem different in the morning, but if not ...

five

Back in Newcastle in 2002, I was wishing I'd never opened the bloody shoebox. I'd managed not to think of what happened for years, always determined to put the whole episode out of my mind. I'd pretended even to myself that it never did happen.

Now these relics of the past were forcing me to remember.

Had things seemed different in the morning after that first night with the Durrants? I couldn't remember. Only that the night was numbingly cold. There was a fireplace, but it had evidently not been used for years. The floorboards were bare except for a small rug in front of the dressing table and I could feel cold air through the cracks. I went to bed wearing all my clothes to try to keep warm.

I'd woken to the sun shining through the light curtain. I could hear the sound of waves breaking on rocks. It was bright morning and there was work to do. I was also hungry. I'd forgotten to wind my wristwatch and it had stopped. There'd been an alarm clock ticking on the bedside table but its loud chatter in the night had made it impossible to get to sleep. I'd pushed it under the mattress so I couldn't hear it.

Hilda had said there'd be hot water in the morning for a bath. I got up, uncomfortable in yesterday's rumpled clothes.

As I moved, I felt a ladder race up my leg from the hole I'd torn in my tights last night coming up the drive. The rescued alarm clock said nine o'clock, but it had stopped. It was set to go off at 7.30. I remembered that I'd heard the shrill ring but then it was so dark that I thought it must be the middle of the night, and had gone back to sleep. It would be just my luck to miss breakfast when I was so hungry. Just as well I was already dressed, laddered tights notwithstanding. I could leave the bath and fresh clothes till later. I didn't usually wear much make-up and once I'd flicked my fingers through my short, mousy hair I thought I would pass muster if no one looked at my legs, which they probably would because of my miniskirt and high heels.

The clock in the hall struck ten as I reached the bottom of the stairs. I listened for voices, but heard nothing. I opened a door into a large room with lofty casement windows over-looking a garden and the sea beyond. The room smelled slightly musty, as though it had not been used for some time. I turned back and found another door off the hall.

At last I found the dining room. A dark mahogany table in the centre was set with three places. On a matching side-board a series of dishes were being kept hot over chafing dishes. There was a smell of melted wax. Hilda Durrant stood stiffly behind a high-backed dining chair at one end of the table, facing the door. Another woman, not as tall but much broader, stood behind a chair at the other end, her back to me. She turned her head at the sound of the door opening, and my first impression was that she could not be related to Hilda. This woman had the head and expression of an elderly mastiff dog, heavy and impassive, with the almost-splendid folds of her jutting chin disappearing into a high-necked black blouse which looked like one of those broad leather collars people buy especially for bulldogs.

She was looking at me, but it seemed to me that she did not register seeing me. But then she smiled and shifted her weight so that she seemed to grow taller, straighter, now unmistakably an elderly version of the young Patience in Cecil Durrant's sketch.

'Come in,' she said, 'come in and we'll say grace so we can sit down. I hope everything hasn't got too cold.' She looked at me and again I got the feeling that she didn't really see me. Her eyes looked like large grey-grained stones in Victorian mourning rings.

There was a tension I didn't understand in the room. I wondered if I had interrupted them in a quarrel, but then I realized that they had simply been waiting for me to come down, and each blamed the other for my lateness. They had stood there all that time, waiting. I was now painfully conscious of my short skirt and ripped tights. I felt horribly embarrassed. I started to back out of the room, not knowing how to apologize or excuse what was obviously a serious breach of good manners. But Hilda forestalled me.

'This is your place,' she said, pointing at the third chair drawn up to the table.

'Oh, I'm so sorry,' I said, 'I never dreamed.... You should've gone ahead without me.'

Hilda put a finger to her lips to demand silence. 'Will you say grace?' she asked Patience.

Patience intoned something under her breath. 'Amen,' she finished, and we sat down. I heard Patience sigh with relief.

'I'm so sorry,' I said again, 'my wristwatch stopped. You shouldn't have waited.'

'It would be unthinkable to be so rude to any guest in our house, Miss Weaver,' Hilda said.

'Frances, please,' I said. She ignored this. She held up a silver coffee pot, poured a cup of coffee and handed it to me. It was plainly cold.

'Patience starts work at nine every morning. I'm sure you will remember that in future,' Hilda said.

'I'm so sorry,' I said. 'I'm afraid the journey caught up with me and I overslept.'

'Oh, no, it's for us to apologize,' Patience said. 'Hilda put an alarm clock in your room to wake you, but it obviously failed to go off.' Again that queer blank stare. She could be blind, I thought. 'She must have forgotten to wind it,' she added with an unamused smile.

Hilda fiddled nervously with a large brooch against the pale grey silk at her throat, a starburst of tiny diamonds set in silver around a fiery black opal. She seemed distressed that I had been made to feel embarrassed.

Patience was still smiling. She had a kind face when she smiled – not that Hilda hadn't, she, too, had a very sweet expression and she smiled a lot. And yet I did not see Hilda as kind. She had very big, long teeth and there was something about her smile that gave the impression that she might bite. I looked from one sister to the other, both smiling, both regarding me with friendly indulgence in spite of my inadvertent flouting of their routine, in spite of the cold stewed coffee we were all trying to drink with an appearance of enjoyment. Hilda tipped the brooch again, making the black opal flash. Watching them together, I couldn't help feeling there was something tormented about Hilda, something weird, as though she knew there was a Dorian Gray-type portrait of her hidden somewhere, which revealed her real self as a werewolf or something more sinister, but that no one would ever find it.

Patience swallowed the coffee in her cup with no sign that it tasted like wet ashes. She got up and began to take the lids off the chafing dishes. This was a noisy business, for she was clumsy. I noticed her big powerful hands, real gardeners' tools of hands. 'Help yourself,' she said, 'you must be hungry.'

'No,' I said. I hadn't the face to delay them any longer. 'No, I'm not hungry, thank you.'

Hilda folded her napkin and stood up. 'Well, I expect you're dying to get to work on Father's papers. I'll show you the study and you can see what's there.'

She strode out of the room and I had no choice but to follow her. I had to hurry to keep up as she gave me a galloping guided tour of the ground floor of the house. She pointed out the view of the sea as we rushed through the room I had already walked into by mistake. It was framed by contorted branches of wisteria outside the window.

'We don't use this drawing room so much now,' she said. 'Not at all, in fact. When my parents were alive they entertained a lot. Wadhurst Carpenter would have drunk many after-dinner brandies in here in those days.' She stood staring round at the furniture as though someone else had been living there since she was last here.

I asked, 'Do you remember him well? Wadhurst Carpenter, I mean?'

'Of course, we saw him when he came here,' Hilda said. She hesitated as though she felt she had to be careful what she said. 'But he came to see my father. We never really knew him.' She touched the black opal brooch, twisting it so that the stone looked at me like a disembodied eye.

I had to try to get on a less formal footing with her. 'Perhaps your father was afraid he'd fall in love with one of you,' I said. I realized at once from Hilda's expression that I'd said the wrong thing. I wished I hadn't been so gauche. But then she smiled.

'Our father agreed with you,' she said. 'He was afraid that Mr Carpenter was not a good moral influence on young women. He locked away the manuscript of *The Seeds of Knowledge* so we couldn't read it.'

My God, I thought, they'd have been in their twenties at least by then, they weren't children. I wanted to ask more questions but Hilda seemed eager to change the subject. She ushered me into another room with the same view over the garden and the sea. This was a much smaller room, more cosy, filled with shabby armchairs and shelves of books and photographs. The ashes of a log fire still glowed in the hearth. A sewing basket with skeins of brightly-coloured silks sat like a flower arrangement on a table. Hilda must have been the one working on the elaborate piece of embroidery beside it, the needle stuck into the stitching.

'Patience and I sit in here in the evenings,' she said. 'That is where you will sit.' She pointed to a small sofa near the fireplace, between two particularly worn armchairs. Hilda indicated one of several heavy oil paintings of grave-looking men on the walls. 'That's a portrait of our father,' she said. 'He was a fine figure of a man, don't you think so?'

I met the glazed gaze of the lined face in the portrait. There was a surprisingly sardonic expression in the greenish eyes. The bright red beard looked defiant. Cecil Durrant seemed to be staring mockingly at a line of whiskered men in military uniform on the wall opposite. Hilda saw me notice these.

'My mother's family,' she said. 'They tended to be generals.' That was where the nose came from, then, the mother's side.

'Is there a picture of your mother?' I asked.

'My father painted her after they were married. You'll see that in his study. Through here.' Hilda set off again with her long, loping stride.

I tried to remember landmarks, but I was sure I would never find my way round by myself. Except at school and some Oxford colleges, I'd never been used to anything except the small domestic arrangements of English suburbia. A dog started to bark somewhere far off. A door banged. I thought of the young red-headed woman who had opened the door to me last night. Did she live here with the sisters, was she a housekeeper? There was a lot of work to do in the house for one servant. Perhaps she was married and her husband did the gardening.

'This way,' Hilda said, already leading the way into another passage.

What was I doing wondering about how they coped? I was there to work. All I should have been interested in was what went on under this roof more than forty years ago, when Wadhurst Carpenter was a regular visitor, and a potential danger to young women.

'It's a wonderful house,' I said as I briefly caught up with Hilda when she paused to examine a black beetle playing dead on the polished wood floor. 'There's a lot to do, though. Do you find it difficult to get help?'

'Help?' Hilda asked. 'Why should we need help?' She picked up the beetle and moved on.

'I meant in the house. Servants.' I was struggling to keep up.

'Oh, I see, staff? A woman comes in from the village. And we can get temporary people if we need them. They're glad enough of the work.'

'No one lives in, then?'

Hilda frowned, puzzled by the questions. 'No,' she said. 'As a family we've always kept ourselves to ourselves.' She opened the door of another room, 'This is my father's study,' she said.

Cecil Durrant's study looked as though he had only just left it. It seemed to me that there was even a faint smell of pipe tobacco in the air, but that was surely whimsy. There were well-thumbed books on his desk, bristling with torn pieces of paper as markers. A pile of papers spilled out of a half-closed drawer. A desk diary lay open on the blotter. The left-hand page was covered in a close scrawl of black ink. The right-hand page was blank. I looked at the date at the top: 22 February 1935.

'That's the day he died,' Hilda said. 'He kept a diary all his life, never missed a day. You'll find that he often mentions Wadhurst Carpenter coming here, but I'm afraid you'll have to wade through a lot of jottings which won't mean much to you in order to get to them.' She was turning the black opal brooch at her throat, pulling the pin against the silk of her blouse.

'I'm looking forward to it,' I said. 'I'm sure your father will really make Wadhurst Carpenter come to life for me. His friendship with your father is the nearest thing I've come across in his life to a personal relationship.'

Hilda gave me a searching look and smiled a little smile as though she pitied me. My heart sank; I was overwhelmed by a horrible certainty that there was nothing here for me, that the whole trip was a hiding to nothing.

'I hope you find him helpful then,' Hilda said. She sounded so sad that I turned to look at her. 'My father, I mean. It seems such a waste, all that work he did, and now no one even knows his paintings. He was a wonderful man, a genius. We were such a happy family.' There was a silence. I could think of nothing to say. Then Hilda shook her head.

'I must go,' she said, 'this won't get the potatoes peeled, will it? I'll leave you to it. We lunch at one. You'll hear the gong at quarter to. I'm sure that will give you time to get to the table on time.' Perhaps I was wrong, but there seemed a hint of a threat in her voice as she said this.

'What about the old diaries? They might be helpful.'

'Oh,' Hilda said, 'I hardly think so. I'm sure my father would have destroyed anything personal as he started each new year. He was a very private man. If he didn't, my mother did.'

It was so clear that she thought I'd overstepped some mark that I didn't pursue the subject. I'd have to come back to it later, when I'd gained her trust.

Left alone, I moved about the room, exploring. Once Hilda had gone I felt immediately comfortable here as I didn't in any of the other rooms I'd been in. I tried to think why this should be so, finally deciding that here there was none of the impression of female long-suffering that seemed to haunt the rest of the house, an aura of disappointment and women unfulfilled.

But there was a woman in the room. The study wall was dominated by Cecil Durrant's portrait of his wife. Against a dark background of trees, dressed in black velvet, she was a vivid and indomitable little figure standing as though with a sword drawn for battle. I found myself thinking how much he must have loved her. I wasn't sure what made me think so, for the portrait was outwardly formal, even cool. But he'd made her look like a saint, or a Crusader, almost as though his marriage was a form of worship, more than ordinary love, something that kept him on the brink of fear.

I turned away from the portrait, finding it discomforting. The window looked out over a shrubbery of bamboo and dense laurel bushes. I imagined Cecil Durrant painting at this window, with nothing in that variation on the theme of green to distract his mind's eye from the sketches of sun and sand and desert sky he had brought back with him from his travels.

I caught a sudden movement among the bamboos, a flash of tawny red and white. I saw a blank, pale face, an old tweed coat tied with a dog lead, the autumn red hair. No sooner had I recognized the young woman from last night than she had disappeared again like a ghost into the bushes. I wondered if I had imagined seeing her. Ghosts don't walk in daylight, I told myself. Or do they?

I sat down at Cecil Durrant's desk. The chair squeaked a little as I leaned back in it. The steely painted eyes of Mrs Durrant seemed to accuse me. But I had a right to be here. I bent forward and opened a drawer. It was crammed with papers, apparently letters. There was also a penknife, a tobacco pouch, a few used pipe cleaners. Also many faded sepia photographs of stocky old men with beards and women dressed as if for a costume museum. Among a dusty collection of buttons and old, rolled-up, tubes of paint I found a key.

I tried it in the desk drawers but it didn't fit. It was too big for the cupboard against the wall opposite the window, and for the sideboard stacked with books. Self-mockingly, I played out the scene as an intrepid detective might in a television series, tapping the bookcases for secret panels, pulling on decorative drawer handles on the davenport and the writing desk, tilting the pictures away from the wall expecting a hidden safe.

I found what I was looking for beside the portrait of Caroline Durrant, hidden by a curtain designed to be pulled across to protect the portrait from the sun. Except there was no sun in this room. Perhaps there had been when Cecil Durrant worked here, before the laurels raised their impenetrable screen.

What I found wasn't really a safe, rather a secret cupboard set into the wall. The key opened it.

I don't know what I was expecting. The atmosphere in the house, not quite sinister but somehow secretive, led me to hope for something between a cache of treasure or a dagger stained with long-dried blood. It was actually an anti-climax when the cupboard held only a collection of diaries. I knew he wouldn't have destroyed them. People didn't write diaries only to destroy them, even if Hilda thought they did. But she must know that; she'd probably thought I'd never find them.

I pulled out several volumes, a uniform series of leather-bound tomes with the year marked in gilt on the spines. The first I picked out was 1909. Too early, probably, for mentions of Wadhurst Carpenter, but that didn't seem to matter now. I opened it. A yellowed piece of paper fluttered to the floor. I picked it up, not sure if it had fallen out of the diary or from a stack of papers on the desk. I glanced at the spidery scrawl. At first I thought it was a letter but as I read on I realized it was a poem.

Hilda my darling my baby dear
This day ends the fourth and begins the fifth year.
Happy day how I would that dear Mummum were here
With my Hilda and Patience or I with you there.
At the table methinks I can see

Your very own little plumpuddy,
With four almonds clear each one for a year.
A piece for Patience, a piece for Mummum,
The rest for little you, and none for Babbu.
Oh how I wish I could be
With you in the garden or by the sea.
But I send a thousand loves, hugs and kisses today
With the little red book for my Hilda's birthday.
Little Baby True I write this for you. Again I kiss you.
May we all see many happy birthdays together
And never more go away from each other.

Babbu

I read the poem over again. It was hard to reconcile the Cecil
Durrant who'd written this doggerel to his little daughter on
her birthday with the man as I pictured him – the loner, the
visionary, the man of action. Where was the strict elderly
paterfamilias with his young wife and children, the disciplinarian who'd locked away Wadhurst Carpenter's great work
in case his daughters saw it and were corrupted? What did
this little poem have to say about a middle-aged recluse who
spent his life avoiding his own kind in foreign lands, and
thought of nothing but his vocation as a painter and guru of
patriotic morality? I couldn't help smiling at the thought of
how outraged Hilda would be to hear her father described as
a guru, but then she probably wouldn't know what the word
meant. I opened the diary at random and started to read the
densely-written, old-fashioned prose.

six

The entry was for 13 September 1913:

It is now upward on three months since Patience and Hilda were judged to be in good health enough at last to attend school. This long breach has proved often irksome in particular to our elder daughter, Patience, but dear Mummum and I think before all else of our little ones, and their health is best where we are there to guard them against the damage that can be done to the young at the hands of well-meaning but mistaken government. Today this truth has been borne in upon me, with which I reproach myself.

Patience at last persuaded myself and dear Mummum that she should go to school and study some subjects of educational value, though we could not countenance others. She is more wilful than her younger sister, and would not be gainsaid. So be it, needs must she try her wings. She must learn for herself that the commonplace school teacher is a dangerous weapon dedicated to destroy the joy of knowledge.

Alas, how I reproach myself for the lowering of my guard which has brought my little one into danger. This afternoon I asked her to repeat what she had learned in the lessons, to find that my darling child had been laid open to the work of a lurid romance by a woman named Brontë, and scarcely part of the serious study of our English literature. It seems that my little one, and, with her other fresh young minds, are inflamed by this unsuitable material and are indeed led frivolously to question moral truths which are constant. Patience shall not go to school again. I myself will undertake the teaching of both our little ones. They will flourish in freedom from formal schooling. There is a simplicity and, so to say, rigidity and standing-up dignity of personal life which will carry a man through everything. Patience shall learn that it is only study of the best minds and thoughts of our great British nation which brings enlightenment. I alone will provide the opportunity of that study unadulterated by contact with what is dross and false.

15 September 1913:
A letter from the Gallery turns down the idea of a small exhibition of new paintings. The tone of this letter is cool, to the point that I am led to suspect that the writer knows nothing of my work. In the long meanwhile money problems press.

25 September 1913:
Charles Ogilvy suggests that I should let this house for a modest rental and take dear Mummum and the little ones to Italy for the winter where we may live simply and without extravagance. He knows of a friend who might be able to help bring about such an arrangement

should I wish it. Ogilvy cannot find a buyer for the Nejd paintings. They are, he claims, out of fashion.

Had the French Impressionists in 1909 already made Cecil Durrant a back number? I didn't know enough about the fashions in art to be sure. Anyway, it was not really his painting technique that had inspired Wadhurst Carpenter, it was the moral philosophy in his message.

As to why, that was one of the questions to which I must find an answer.

seven

Alone in my room that night, I wrote to Alison:

How's the leg? I don't know when I'll get the chance to post this letter, which will be a positive journal by the time it gets to you. How I wish you were here with me. Really, this is the weirdest place, you'd love it, it's like one of those old horror stories where nothing is what it seems to be. On the surface, it's a beautiful old house covered in ancient gnarled creepers, set on the cliffs above a creek where the waves crash in and break like cracking whips when the wind's blowing, which it always seems to be. From the drawing room you can see great dark rolling banks of rain coming across the bright silver sea, and then in the evening there are these incredible sunsets on the horizon, all black and fiery red and that glittery green of cats' eyes. And yet I can't get it out of my head that the house has a sinister life of its own. It's full of dark corners and creaking stairs and unused rooms no one ever goes into, and the gardens are a tangle of overgrown evergreen bushes with poisonous-looking black and red berries and a smell of rotting leaves. Mind you, I haven't ventured far from the house yet. There's something about the place which makes me feel I shouldn't be there, as if it's some-where human beings aren't welcome. Only Hilda, the younger of the sisters, goes out into the wild part of the grounds, but she always takes the dogs with her. There are four of them, a cairn terrier, two mongrels and a Pekinese, all maimed in some way, and when they're out walking they rush around on three legs or whatever, and those that have tails wag them, all barking as though they can see evil spirits everywhere. Actually I'd back Hilda against any evil spirit, there's something really witchy about her, more than simply having a long nose and whispy grey hair and walking about as though she's sweeping along on a broomstick. She's got all sorts of familiars, too, like raggedy old crows and toads in damp, dark places in the garden, and she has great big hands like a strangler's. Of course this is nonsense, she's a sweet old lady who smells of Ponds cold cream and lavender talc and wouldn't hurt a fly, but this place is so isolated from the rest of the world it plays tricks with the imagination.

Actually, Hilda puts me to shame. She's so full of energy, like a hiker, the rate she moves. I still get the feeling, though, that even she doesn't like to go too far away from the house. At times I suspect she's afraid if she did go too far, the vegetation would swallow the path by the time she came back and she'd lose her way and miss the gong! Oh, that gong, it rules all our lives!

I can just see you thinking I've caught a bad dose of whimsy since I came to Ireland, but fear not, it's simply that I've been spending too much time in the company of two old ladies and no one else. It's as though they've got stuck in a previous century and don't know that things have changed. If the Durrants suddenly found themselves in the middle of Newcastle on a Saturday morning, they'd probably think they'd landed on the moon. They look at my skirts as though they think I'm dressed in costume. At least, Hilda does; Patience just stares as though she can't believe her eyes.

As a matter of fact, they look a bit outlandish themselves, even in Ireland where they're not exactly unfamiliar with the English. I've told you how tall they are, and Patience is big, built like a riveter, but at the same time they behave like small women, you know, really girlie. They're the sort who can't talk about anything except it's a 'dear little this' or a 'darling little that'. Since they never talk about anything except their pets and the garden, it all gets a bit much. But you'd expect them to be a bit odd, wouldn't you, shut away here for decades with only one old woman who comes in every day to cook? And then there's a queer redheaded creature like something out of Burne-Jones or Rossetti who hovers in the bushes and seems to be some kind of gardener and may or may not be mentally deficient. Or maybe there isn't. She could easily be a figment of my imagination.

The witchy old cook cycles away every evening and honestly I get the feeling when I see her go that she's like a messenger from our besieged fort trying to get through hostile Red Indians to bring the US Seventh Cavalry to the rescue. And of course she never gets through, because no one comes here that I've seen, no one at all, and she's back in the morning and everything goes on as before.

I like to think of you, back home reading this, thinking I must be going off my head with such fantasies. Why would we need a dispatch rider? Why wouldn't we simply use the telephone? Well, because there isn't a telephone.

And of course there isn't a television. And they don't take a newspaper, either. I know it sounds incredible that people could live like this in the 1960s, but the twentieth century really hasn't ruffled the surface of life at Balcurran House, at least since Cecil Durrant died, it hasn't. The only way the old ladies hear anything about the outside world is on the BBC Nine O'Clock News on what they call the 'wireless'. The three of us sit in the drawing room in the most straight-backed posture I've ever known and Hilda turns on the radio at one minute to nine and we listen as solemnly as if we were at a funeral service in church. When it's over she gets up and turns it off and that's that. No one says anything. They just go into the next step of their routine. I am dispatched to my room, Hilda takes the dogs out for a last walk, and then Patience goes out to lock up, moving like a zombie to a familiar beat.

Seriously, Alison, the Durrants are perfectly ordinary elderly women who've fallen into a rigid routine. I think. But all the same there is something sort of threatening about them, or about this place. Perhaps it's the place that has had an effect on them. Balcurran House seems to me like a chrysalis and everyone here is trapped inside waiting to turn into a butterfly. Or rather, a drab old moth. A mothy old couple. Patience is the husband, and she wears a lot of tweed and what look like men's shirts and she has hands with rough skin like a workman, which I suppose must come from being a plant scientist buried to the elbows in soil. Apparently she was a great sailor, too, and used to go out mackerel fishing on the local fishing boats when she was younger. That's what Hilda says, anyway, though I get the feeling that all that *is a bit too down-to-earth for Patience. If she went to sea, it would be to take off round the world on a sailing ship, or perhaps to the South Pacific after Moby Dick. She often seems kind of dreamy when she's talking to you, as though she's listening to something you can't hear. I think I told you she's got this huge head. I have this fantasy that if she'd ever made her voyage on a four-master to faraway places with strange-sounding names, she would have been the perfect figurehead, with those blind eyes and that jutting profile at the prow pointing ever onward through mountainous waves and into the unknown. Anyway, here at home they're like an old married couple together, the breadwinner and the home-maker and mother. Obviously Hilda's not a mother – they're both in different ways the most virginal virgins I've ever seen – but she calls the maimed pets her little babies as though she really was their mother.... Her poor little babies, that's what she says.*

I tell myself I'm writing to you to take your mind off being laid up. But it's not just that. It sounds too silly for words to say I feel I have to make someone understand how I feel so that I can get on top of it and move on with what I'm doing. I'm uneasy, that's all I can say. I don't know how to act. I can't make sense of the Durrants' life here. It scares me, if you must know. They live by such rigid rules you'd think they were in prison being bossed about by hidden jailers. But at the same time they make me feel that I'm the prisoner and they're the jailers. I tell myself that this is nonsense, that it only feels like that because there's no public transport and no one from outside seems to visit, and they never go anywhere, and they're quite happy, but then it occurs to me that the one form of imprisonment you can volunteer for is in a mental institution and that just makes me feel worse.

There's one bonus from all this, though. I'm beginning to connect with Wadhurst Carpenter. He seems much more real to me now that I have the feeling he and I are the only normal people who've ever stayed in the Durrant household. I found a paragraph in one of Cecil Durrant's diaries yesterday that said W.C. spent an entire autumn evening helping Mrs Durrant, 'our dearest Mummum', plant bulbs in the copse. Not very convincing evidence of sanity, I suppose, but imagine the author of The Seeds of Knowledge *doing that! I've found snaps of him with Patience and Hilda from all those years ago, on the beach and playing with the dogs, that sort of thing. Even in the photographs I get the impression that the sisters weren't at ease. They seem embarrassed simply having fun. I find myself sitting with the two of them in the evening and wondering what my hero made of this family. I can't understand why a man like that, full of life and energy, would want to be here at all. Perhaps he was making mock of them all.*

But then you have to understand the way Patience and Hilda were brought up. I had no idea until the other day. I was trying to make conversation over lunch – meals with them are horrendous, terrifically stiff and formal with no one saying anything except about the weather. Anyway, I made some comment about the village, which of course I've never seen because I've not been out of the house, or at least the grounds, since I got here. And Hilda said to Patience, as though she thought she'd been specially privileged, 'Do you remember how Papa used to call me into his study and say "Today we study geography" and tell me to open the atlas and it always seemed to open at Germany. And I'd sit there staring at the map for an hour or so while he worked away at his desk. Then he'd come over and shut the atlas and say, "There, today you have really learned something," and send me away?'

That seemed weird enough, but do you know, he wouldn't even let them read what they liked at home. They were only allowed to read parts of Chaucer and Spenser and the Bible because the old man thought the way all later writers used the English language was degenerate, over-influenced by Latin. And when I asked if they smuggled in novels to read secretly, Patience said they were never interested in fiction, why waste time reading the nonsense that people make up in their heads because, by definition, it must all be lies?

Obviously, anyway, all that biblical stuff put them off reading because they never seem to read now. I came into the room once and caught Patience sitting with an open magazine glaring at the page but never turning it. She didn't hear me at first, and then she raised her head and smiled. I've worked out she's going blind but she never says a word about it because that would be a sign of weakness.

Honestly, it isn't normal. It isn't natural, either, the way no one visits. There's that old woman who comes in on her bicycle every morning to work in the kitchen, and the fey girl with red hair who flits about in the woods and appears and disappears like a ghost. I haven't placed her yet – if she really exists. I may be seeing things. Oh, God, there's the gong. I'm beginning to feel like a cuckoo clock.

P.S. Tuesday evening:
I realized this morning that I've been at Balcurran House exactly a week. Surely it must be more than that, I feel as though I've been coming into Cecil Durrant's room at 8.45 every day for as long as I can remember.

I can't get over how easily I've become part of what's really a kind of automated life here, but, after all, this isn't so surprising. Daily I read Cecil Durrant's old diaries describing an identical routine; now, decades later, Patience carries on where he left off, and Hilda acts out her mother's days more or less as she did. It isn't surprising that I'm gradually being overcome by the weight of the practice of years. But I think I'm beginning to understand better what Wadhurst Carpenter got out of being here. I know all the photos show him messing around, and he looks really happy, much happier than in the formal pictures the magazines and newspapers of his day used when they mentioned him. I think he came here because it must have been a terrific place to work. He was one of those people always rushing around doing things and going places, but here there wasn't much else he could do except work. That's not what the Durrants want to hear, though. They want to be told that their father is the star. They're constantly asking me what I've found out about the old boy's vital role in creating the famous man. But there's nothing to satisfy them. I've even taken to embroidering the truth a little to give them what they want. You know, if Cecil Durrant mentions going for a walk with Wadhurst Carpenter, or a conversation they had, I'll tell Patience and Hilda that their father advised him what to say, or made up a phrase Wadhurst Carpenter would go on to claim as his own. It keeps them happy for the time being, anyway.

The odd thing is, there are lots of mentions of Wadhurst Carpenter in the early diaries I've been looking at, but then all mention of him seems to stop. I scent the possibility of something interesting, but it's too soon to say anything for certain.

It's fascinating how the Durrant sisters themselves still work. They're old women, yet they take no rest. There's no sign, though, of the results of their labours, at least as far as I can tell. There aren't any visits from experts studying Patience's methods, no learned scientific journals featuring her research, no international telephone calls; indeed, no telephone calls at all, of course, because there isn't a telephone.

Then again, prints of Hilda's paintings don't appear on the walls. She doesn't come in from the garden with interesting flowers or pods to dissect for her meticulous drawings. I know she does 'meticulous paintings' because I've read it in the reference book in the university library at home, but that, and the mentions of the Durrants in an old Who's Who, is all the evidence I have that their work exists at all. And yet Patience works in an office converted from an old stable at the back of the house from 6.30 in the morning to 6.30 at night, Monday to Saturday, breaking for an hour for breakfast and for lunch, half an hour for morning coffee and afternoon tea. Each working day she wears a white overall covering an outfit which is like a uniform, a dark box-pleated skirt, white shirt, and dark blue cardigan. On Sundays the skirt and cardigan are grey.

I haven't seen inside her office, and I've no idea what a botanical scientist's office looks like; I suppose it must be something like an ordinary laboratory. Hilda let drop one day that she's never been inside her sister's workroom either. And Patience hasn't been into the turret room at the top of the house where Hilda paints. I tried to wangle an invitation to Hilda's room by saying what a wonderful view it must have, forgetting that she's a technical painter and probably despises views, although I think Hilda the technician conceals a romantic soul. There's that great big model sailing ship in the hall, for one thing, I'm sure that's down to Hilda.

I wouldn't even hint to Patience that I'd like to see her room. I suppose in a way I can understand the way she feels about her work, but if her sight's going, and I think it is, it would make it worse if I forced her to face that she's losing it. She's the sort who'd do anything to hide it, even down to sitting in her lab all day pretending nothing's changed. It's quite possible, you know. And I've seen her eyes. They look exactly like two glass marbles stuck in her head, not like real eyes at all. She's trying to turn the clock back, pretending that she's got important work to do, and she may be able to believe it as long as she's alone in her own room, or with Hilda, but she must know she can't convince an outsider. It's different for Hilda, because her realm is really the household. She only goes to her turret studio to paint when she's finished in the house.

But think of all those years of unvarying days, how can they stand it? Did they ever think of the world outside, of other lives they could have lived? And yet, I have to admit, in just one week, life at Balcurran House has begun to weave its cocoon around me, too. I sit at Cecil Durrant's desk trying to concentrate on the old man's papers on the lookout for a mention of Wadhurst Carpenter, thinking the sooner I get through this, the sooner I'm on my way out of here. But it's no good, I still feel like Keats and his 'drowsy numbness ... as though of hemlock ...'

Please write back to me, even if it's just to prove that Balcurran House is on the same planet as the real world of Swinging London. You might send me a fiver, too, because although Hilda seems perfectly happy to post my letters for me, I'd like to pay her for the stamps. I start tomorrow on Cecil Durrant's diary for New Year's Day 1915. A bit early for anything about Wadhurst Carpenter, of course, but it may help me understand the Durrants better. I have this strong feeling that Cecil Durrant is the key to Wadhurst Carpenter. A new year, surely a time for reflection or anticipation, some kind of self-relevation from such a devout Christian as Cecil Durrant?

eight

---

1 January 1915:
A bitter day with flakes of snow carried in the easterly
wind. The tern with a broken wing that Hilda, the loving
heart, had brought home for succour, she found dead
this morning in its box. Poor Hildina, her tears were sad
to see. My own work is held up by the condition of some
of my paints, with which the little ones, strictly against
my orders, were playing while confined indoors by the
weather. Now I must await replacements from London,
but the postman will not call today so needs must I find
other ways to occupy the time God in His goodness has
set aside for work.

3 February 1915:
The paints have arrived. My work at last forges ahead.
There is nothing to be said.

2 March 1915:
Our household is in uproar over an incident which may
lead to the dismissal of our faithful Mr and Mrs Fry, the
couple who act as gardener and cook here. They have a
young child, a girl, whom Hilda lately befriended. Now

this rude child has reported to her mother, our servant, that she saw Hilda mistreat, indeed inflict damage upon, one of the birds in the aviary, I think a magpie is in question.

Mrs Fry brought this story to dear Mummum. The Fry child was fetched, in tears, to make the extraordinary claim that in response to her efforts to stop Hilda from hurting this bird, my gentle little daughter made threats against her, saying she would shut her in the woodshed and leave her there until the spiders spun webs over her mouth and eyes to suffocate her, or the ivy grew up around her neck and strangled her.

Dear Mummum did her best to find out from Hilda why the Fry child should tell such lies, but Hilda is as bewildered as we are. I myself, and indeed Mummum too, feel hurt and betrayed that a servant in our home could act as Mrs Fry did, in listening to the lies of a child which were so much to the discredit of our sweet and trustful Hilda. Our darling is, and has been always, marked out from others by her rare compassion and her loving care for all wounded creatures. No doubt the false accuser is driven by natural envy, but I confess that my mind is much disturbed by this incident that I have failed to protect my little daughter from such malice. Mummum saw to it that the Fry child should be punished for her crime, that she must be taught to tell the truth, and that she should in future be prevented from being where she might see or talk to Hilda. The Frys have been told also that if they do not enforce this, they must leave our service. Altogether a most distressing day.

nine

Back in Newcastle now in 2002, I remember across the years the shock of reading that diary entry. I remember how Cecil Durrant's fine sloping script suddenly changed. It became a furious scrawl, rushing across the page with a forward slant which looked as if he were racing to escape demons, the punctuation marks like drops of blood from a wound where he stabbed the paper with his pen.

But what on earth had Hilda done to scare the Fry girl so? What was Hilda's terrible and unnatural cruelty? Because that was what shocked me so much then and still startles me now. Cecil Durrant and 'darling Mummum' could call her a liar, but, so many years later, I believed that stubborn little Fry girl's story. What, when it came down to it, would have given her the idea to make up something so outlandish?

And what had happened afterwards? I wonder now, as I'd wondered when I first read that diary entry, what happened to Hilda, not to the defeated little Fry girl? It's as though I'm back in Cecil Durrant's study, the dark laurels menacing the window, the wind in the bamboo canes in their dense saw-toothed clumps sounding like the clash of swords in battle. Was Hilda sorry, ashamed that other people suffered from what she had done? I'd thought at the time that wasn't how she'd feel. She'd be triumphant. Hadn't she proved her power over the Fry child, who was punished and humiliated and shown to be helpless? I remember asking myself, if I'd discovered that I had power like that, would I have been afraid to use it again? And the young woman I was then had told herself that if she'd been in Hilda's shoes, she wouldn't have been afraid of using it again. She'd have been afraid not to.

So much is coming back to me as I sit on the neat, impersonal new bed in Mum's old room, in the house which I've never felt so much to be home as now when it no longer is. But in my mind's eye, I'm in the dining room at Balcurran House. We have finished breakfast. Hilda and Patience are folding their embossed linen napkins....

'I'm going into town to do the shopping today,' Hilda said. 'Is there any little errand I can do for you, dear?'

'Could I come with you?' I asked. 'I've got a letter to post, and I'd like to see the town while I'm here.'

'You know that you put any letters you have out on the hall table by the model ship and they'll be posted,' Hilda said. 'Don't you trust me to make sure your boyfriend gets your billets-doux?'

I ignored the question. Let them think I had a boyfriend.

Patience said, 'Hilda's an old romantic, posting your letters makes her feel like a go-between. You wouldn't begrudge her that, would you?'

'I don't have any Irish stamps.'

'We have stamps,' Patience said. She had a way of snapping her mouth shut with a little smile which closed a subject then and there.

'You don't think the sightseeing would be better left until you've finished your work?' Hilda said.

I didn't know what to say. I wondered if Hilda had intended to make me feel so acutely that I was a kind of hired hand at Balcurran House. Not simply a hired hand, either, but also someone extremely young placed there for moral guidance like an old-fashioned housemaid.

'I need to cash a cheque,' I said. 'I used all the money I had on the taxi coming here.'

'You won't need money here,' Hilda said. She seemed affronted, for some reason.

'Hilda will post your letter for you,' Patience said. She paused, then added, 'Hilda having to go into Porterstown this afternoon isn't really a chance for you to take a day out, you know. She has a lot to do while she's there, and she's always in a hurry to get through the shopping. I'm afraid you'd be disappointed, too, there's nothing to see, it's only a very small place.'

'Of course,' I said, with as much dignity as I could muster while being treated like a greedy child, 'that's fine. Maybe I'll make the trip one day on my own. Surely there must be a bus from somewhere? Or perhaps I could borrow your car?'

'Oh, dear, I don't think so, it's not insured for anyone except me to drive,' Hilda said. She turned the black opal brooch at her throat so that it caught the light and again seemed to stare at me like a disapproving eye. 'And there isn't any bus. But you misunderstood. I'd be glad to drive you round to show you the area whenever you feel you can spare the time. I know how busy you are, and how keen to get on with the work on your book. You've come all this way to do so, after all.'

I have to admit that she wasn't being unreasonable. I'd gilded the lily often enough when I told them about my exciting research into their father's importance in the making of the modern myth that was Wadhurst Carpenter. At least it passed the time over those long awkward meals when I told them how Cecil Durrant had explained the use of the ablative absolute to his pupil. Wadhurst Carpenter was famous for his use of the ablative absolute in *The Seeds of Knowledge*. I just let Cecil Durrant's daughters give the old man the credit, that's all. It was what they wanted to hear. In fact there was evidence in the diaries that Cecil Durrant had tried to get his pupil to abandon his Latinate syntax and write simple English. Patience and Hilda didn't want to be told that their father had almost made the great writer into an ordinary hack.

Then Patience smiled an approving smile at her sister, and I realized that Hilda was offering an apology of a kind. But I could see from Hilda's face that she did not know what she had done to offend. I felt embarrassed. I wasn't sure what was going on here. And then I looked at that shy, sweet, slightly drooping old lady and I couldn't believe I could suspect her of anything at all, even a fleeting unkind thought. There must be something the matter with me, not her. Is that why I was so touchy? She must have thought I was being pushy wanting to go with her, that was all. After all, we weren't friends, our connection was strictly business.

Hilda smiled at me, a sweet smile. 'I can see we're going to have to lock you into Father's room to keep your nose to the grindstone,' she said. 'You young people are all the same, a short attention span – isn't that what you call it?'

I went to my room to fetch my letter to Alison. When I came down Hilda was waiting in the courtyard at the back of the house, seated behind the wheel of a battered little car which seemed to be shaking with fever as the engine ticked over. I saw the Ford logo on the front of the car but that vehicle wasn't like any Ford I'd ever seen, it must be something they'd made when they were starting out, as an experiment. Suddenly Newcastle, even England, seemed a long way away. I handed the letter to Hilda through the car window. I noticed she'd taken off the black opal brooch. Perhaps she was afraid of putting temptation in the way of the simple peasants of Porterstown. She put the car in gear and took off with a spitting of gravel. She skidded as she sped wildly out of the yard onto a road which seemed to run along the top of a cliff. It was the first time I'd seen the courtyard gates open. The road outside seemed to hang out into the open sky.

I heard Hilda, out of sight, revving the car engine as though she were driving at Silverstone. Then the sound was lost as its high-pitched whine mingled with the shrieks of seabirds. She was going much too fast on that twisting road. 'Well,' I said aloud, 'I don't give much for Alison's chances of ever receiving that letter.' And I laughed. It wasn't the old-lady way I'd expected Hilda to drive.

'Oh, isn't that Miss Hilda for you?' said a voice behind me, 'Doesn't Miss Hilda always drive at top speed? It's a very quiet road, thanks be, and there's seldom any traffic, though for certain she's sent a few sheep off the cliffs in her time?'

I turned to see the old cook standing behind me, her hands on her hips.

'The car looks as if it's taken a few knocks, too,' I said, and smiled to show I didn't mean any real criticism of Hilda.

'You'll be the young lady from England come to study the Master's old papers?' the cook said. I found her accent difficult to understand. The woman was probably in her seventies, but only her wispy white hair and gnarled, arthritic hands betrayed old age. The skin on her round red face was smooth and unlined.

I smiled at her, disconcerted by the way she stated facts as questions. I wasn't sure if she expected answers. 'I've seen you cycle away from the house in the evenings,' I said. 'Do you live in the village? I've wanted to tell you what a good cook you are, but I don't even know your name.'

'Molly Dunn,' the woman said. She began to walk towards the back door of the house and I followed her.

'I've worried about you sometimes when the weather's bad, cycling all that way,' I said. 'Doesn't it bother you in the winter?'

Molly Dunn grunted, which I took to mean that she thought all young women, particularly young English women, were soft and not like the young girls in her day.

'Isn't it a question of going or staying?' she said after a while. 'And there's not many round these parts would want to spend a night in Balcurran House. I like a bit of life, you know, the traffic and the old men coming out of the pub at nights, it makes me feel safe. Isn't it a deal too quiet up here of a night to be natural? And shouldn't I be the one to know, having lived here long enough myself as a little one?'

'You lived here as a child?' I asked. 'So you remember Mrs Durrant? You've been here all that time?'

'Bless you, I've been here all my life as long as I remember,' Molly said. 'I remember the Master and the Mistress, and Miss Patience and Miss Hilda from when we were little ones.'

I seemed to have found the way to conversation with Molly now, you had to ask her a question and she answered, otherwise she asked herself the questions and didn't give any answer.

'Are you married, Molly?' I asked. 'What does your husband do round here?'

'Dunn, that's my married name,' Molly said. 'He was drowned, poor Dunn, this forty years gone, out on the fishing boats. A Corkman, he was, from down the coast aways. But I was born here, and I stayed. I'm Molly Fry as was.'

So, I thought, hearing the name Fry, this must be the child who had so incensed Cecil Durrant with her unlikely tales about Hilda? I looked at the old cook with interest, but I knew I must tread carefully.

'You know I'm studying Mr Durrant's papers for a book I'm writing?' I said. 'About Wadhurst Carpenter, who used to come here. Do you remember him?'

'And why wouldn't I remember such a fine gentleman?' she said. Was she deliberately keeping her expression blank, or did she really have nothing to say?

'I'd love to talk to you about the old days here,' I said. 'Could you spare me time for that?'

'Well, I don't know about that,' Molly said. 'I wouldn't want to say anything untoward.'

'Oh, nothing like that,' I said. 'But, you know, Cecil Durrant was an important man, and you can probably tell more about him than anyone, being part of the family as you were, but also seeing him from outside, if you see what I mean? It's difficult for the daughters or wife of a man like that to see him as he really was, don't you think? But someone like you, a bright girl with experience of life, who'd be better placed than you to know the little things that would make him come to life to a reader?'

'And what kind of little things would those be?' Molly Dunn was still suspicious.

I tried to think of something which might get the old woman to start remembering. 'Oh, any stories your mother and father told about him? What was his favourite meal? Did he play with the children? What were the children like? Who came here to visit them, apart from Wadhurst Carpenter? What did they talk about when he was here? Anything you can think of.' The direct questions again seemed to put her at ease.

'Well, I remember a lot, of course. I was brought up in this house, I was part of the family then.' I heard a wistful note in Molly's voice and understood that she was remembering a time when she'd been happy.

'That's wonderful,' I said, trying to be encouraging. 'You could be so much help. We could just chat about how it was when Mr Durrant was alive? And then, after he died, with Mrs Durrant? And what about a cup of tea?'

Molly's round face cracked into a smile. 'I've cakes in the oven to see to,' she said, 'but if you'll come in the kitchen...?'

It was warm in the kitchen, cosy with the smell of baking and the sun shining on neat lines of earthenware jars and old-fashioned utensils. I'd seen the same sort of thing in rural life museums back home.

'It's wonderful,' I said, looking round. 'It's the kind of homey kitchen people like me, who live in towns, read about as part of country life, but I never thought they really existed outside books and magazines.'

Molly spooned tea leaves into a big brown pot. She evidently liked her tea strong.

'You must've known Mrs Durrant pretty well?' I said. 'You know, I've got a picture of Mr Durrant in my mind, and I can imagine Patience and Hilda as girls, but I can't even conceive what Mrs Durrant was like. Patience and Hilda talk about their father all the time, but they hardly mention her. And there's not much about her in Cecil Durrant's papers so far.'

Molly broke a biscuit she had just taken from the oven and gave a little nod of satisfaction. 'She was a real lady was Mrs Durrant,' Molly said. 'Little thing, she was, they all towered over her, but didn't she keep them all in order?'

'She must've been very beautiful,' I said, 'there's the painting, and I've seen some photos, she always looks beautiful.'

'Like a jewel, she was, a glowing dark gemstone,' Molly said. 'And she had a lovely voice, low-pitched, and it could make you shiver her just asking the price of beef. Didn't she know the price of everything, she did so, and came down checking the weights when the grocer delivered. No one got away with anything, she made sure of that.'

'What did she do with her time here?' I asked. 'It must've been lonely for her here sometimes, Mr Durrant working all the time.'

'She had a beautiful singing voice, as wouldn't Josef Locke himself have paid good money to hear her?' Molly said. 'And she played the piano. Sure, she did everything well did Mrs Durrant. She painted pictures and her needlework was lovely. She tried to teach Miss Patience and Miss Hilda, but they never took to it. Not singing, nor the piano, nor poetry either. They were little savages, the both of them. Miss Patience always out in a boat or netting the prawns along the shore, and Miss Hilda, although she didn't do those rough things, she was wild underneath somehow, as though she didn't ever think of the consequences of things.'

'I don't understand,' I said. 'What do you mean?'

'Well,' Molly said, and then took some time before she went on, as though she was trying to explain something she didn't really understand but knew existed, like the love of God or electricity. 'Well,' she said, 'there was one time she took in a bird with a broken wing, and she set the bone and looked after it, getting up night after night every three hours to feed it, and then one day she decided it should be able to fly again and she tossed it off the cliff and it wasn't mended and it just fell into the sea.'

There was a short silence. Then I said, 'What did she do? She must have felt terrible?'

'No, that's the queer thing,' Molly said, 'she didn't. She just brushed her hands together to clean them from the feathers and she said something as though she blamed the bird for wasting her time not getting better as quickly as it should.' Molly paused and then added, 'I remember thinking then, innocent little child that I was, that it was a queer way for her to be, I thought she'd break her heart with love of that bird, the way she'd nursed it.'

'Did anyone know? Did you tell anyone about it?' I was trying to probe without being too intrusive. This must have been the incident that had upset Cecil Durrant so much he'd nearly thrown the Frys out of the house over it.

Molly shook her head, not denying anything, she was simply looking back to something long ago that she hadn't understood then nor made sense of since. She looked sad, and didn't answer directly. 'That saved their lives, poor bird,' she said at last.

'Saved their lives?'

'It's so long ago, I'd almost forgotten. It was the Shinners, you see, they wouldn't have anything to do with madness. When they were coming to the house, as they were, didn't my Da tell Paddy Boyle about Miss Hilda doing that and Paddy took it that she was mad, so they never came to

Balcurran. Mad was one thing, but wasn't a mad child too much to take? So they never came.'

I didn't know what she was talking about. 'The Shinners?' I asked.

'The boys,' she said. 'During the Troubles.'

'Did the Durrants ever know that?'

Molly gave me a pitying look at my stupidity. 'Bless you,' she said, 'but the Shinners thought he was mad too and had passed it to her in his blood. How else to explain a man who was as unnatural as the Master in the life he led? He wasn't like the other West Britons. He never in his life rode to hounds, nor sat astride a horse that I ever saw.'

'So your father saved them from—' I'd been going to say 'the terrorists', but I suddenly wondered if that would offend Molly. I wished I knew more about Irish history, it hadn't even occurred to me that she might be a Catholic.

She finished the thought for me. 'They'd have been burned out for sure if they weren't kilt,' she said with some satisfaction, though whether at the Durrant's intended fate long ago or their escape from it, I couldn't be sure.

'What did Mrs Durrant make of it?'

Molly seemed suddenly to wake out of her nostalgic trance. 'Of what Miss Hilda did?' she asked. 'Sure, didn't she tell Miss Hilda she should learn a lesson from it, she should see that if something was worth doing it was worth doing well or not at all.' Molly paused. She seemed in retrospect to find this most puzzling of all. 'Mrs Durrant, you see, she set the standards,' she added.

'What do you mean, set the standards?'

'Well, what I mean is … it was like with them playing the piano or singing, the little girls weren't encouraged to do things where they weren't good at what she was trying to teach them. She didn't believe there was any point in doing something for fun or their own pleasure. I think myself that Miss Patience would have enjoyed her piano playing if she'd been allowed to go on with it, but she wasn't, she wasn't good enough. I sometimes think now that was a pity. A little music might be a consolation now.'

So Molly Dunn thought there was something wrong with Patience. Did Molly know the poor old thing was going blind and trying to hide it?

'Why does she need consolation?' I asked. 'Why do you think that?'

Molly Dunn didn't answer. She went on as though I hadn't interrupted, 'She was a stickler, was Mrs Durrant.'

'Jesus!' I said, and I saw Molly cringe at the blasphemy, 'she sounds terrifying. What about Mr Durrant? What happened when he didn't measure up?'

'If I understand you, Miss, Mr Durrant was above all that. There was his work, that was all, that was what they called a sacred trust. He used to talk to Mr Carpenter about that. They'd shut themselves away in the Master's study for hours. I took them coffee in there some mornings and I'm glad enough I couldn't understand a word they said, all about heathen savages and wilderness places. Mrs Durrant didn't have anything to do with his work, of course, except in so far as they all lived for it in a way, it was the point of their lives, the lot of them, and my poor Da too who depended on them. And she did help the Master with the social side of things, of course, when people came down to talk business to him. But she was very strict.'

'Strict?' I was puzzled. 'How could Mrs Durrant be strict with people who came to see her husband about his work?'

'Well, some of the people who wanted to talk to him, they

weren't suitable to her mind, not with young girls in the house. There was a well-known painter who wanted to paint Mr Durrant's picture once, a famous man from London he was, known all over the world, but she wouldn't have it. Wouldn't have him in the house, because he was a man who had divorced his wife and taken another woman without benefit of the church, if you get my meaning. No offence meant, but if she had heard you just now taking the Lord's name in vain, you'd be out of the house and never asked again.'

'I'm sorry.'

'Bless you, never mind me, but Mrs Durrant, she'd travelled among the heathens, Mahometans and the like, she knew the value of her religion. Or so she said. Mr Durrant said the same.'

'But it would've been good for Cecil Durrant, wouldn't it, to be painted by a famous man and be hung in one of the big galleries?'

'I dare say it would have been, but that painter fellow didn't come up to standard to come in the house, not to Mrs Durrant's standard.'

'She sounds quite a character.'

'She was so, and never changed, even when she was an old lady. I remember there was another young lady came once, after Mr Durrant died, to take some of his paintings with her back to Dublin, or maybe it was America, to collect for a book. She was a foreigner, anyway. Well, Mrs Durrant had the habit then, when she could still get about, of walking down the drive to the big gate when someone was coming here, to meet their taxi and open the gate for them. She used to sit and wait for visitors for hours sometimes, the taxi drivers got lost a lot, you see. If you ask me they used to do it so as they could charge the foreigners more for taking them on a wild goose chase.'

'What happened with the young woman?'

'Oh, yes, well, this young lady she went back where she came from and she published the book and she wrote in the book about how she had come to Balcurran House to choose the paintings and how Mrs Durrant had waited for her at the end of the drive. The young woman thought it was the height of good manners that Mrs Durrant did that herself, and made her feel welcome. But Mrs Durrant took offence. After she read what that young woman said in the book no one was allowed to mention the young woman's name in the house again. Mrs Durrant never forgave her. I recall much later that she wanted to do another book about the Master's work, but Mrs Durrant would never speak to her because of what she'd done.' Molly poured more tea. There was a pause.

'What exactly had she done?' I asked at last. I felt I had missed something obvious. To my relief, Molly laughed.

'Blessed if I know,' she said, 'all I know, Mrs Durrant never forgave her for putting it down in public print.'

'It can't have been easy for Patience and Hilda, when they were young. What happened if Mrs Durrant didn't like their friends?'

'They didn't have friends,' Molly said.

'But they must have had friends? They must have gone out and had other children here. What about parties and tennis and picnics in the summer?'

'Oh, no, nothing like that. They didn't have time to waste on that kind of thing. Besides, there weren't suitable children for them to see.'

Molly, 'the Fry child', I knew, had been unsuitable. I couldn't tell from Molly's expression whether or not she admired the Durrants' single-mindedness. I was trying to frame another question to learn more without putting Molly on guard, when she added, 'They weren't like other young ladies. They'd always kept themselves to themselves, you understand, that was the way they'd been brought up. And Miss Hilda at least was delicate.'

'You mean she really was ill? Why, did she have TB or something?'

'No, it wasn't that. It was that she couldn't be excited.'

'It sounds to me as though she must have been lonely,' I said.

'Oh, no, she and Miss Patience were always company for each other. Only Miss Hilda had to be protected specially.'

I knew that Molly wanted to change the subject but I felt I had to persist. 'Excited mentally, you mean. She really did have mental trouble?' I thought of the bird.

'No, no, it was her nerves. She suffered from her nerves.' Molly was struggling to explain something she obviously didn't understand and never had understood. There was a sudden scraping sound from outside the door. Molly smiled. 'Ah, here she is,' she said.

The kitchen door was thrust open and the elusive red-haired girl from my first night burst in. She kicked off mud-laden boots as she came. She pulled off a ragged coat and revealed a thick knitted jumper and baggy corduroy trousers. Her red hair caught the light and gleamed like red gold. This Pre-Raphaelite creature didn't give me a glance.

'Death On The Roads gone out, has she?' she said to Molly.

'Here's our Jenny then,' Molly said. 'Take no notice of her fun, she means Miss Hilda. She won't get in a car with Miss Hilda the way she drives, isn't that so, Jenny?'

I smiled. 'You let me in the night I arrived,' I said. 'I've seen you around since. I'm pleased to meet you.'

Jenny ignored me. She had caught sight of the tray of biscuits on the table and grabbed a handful. I'd taken her to be a teenager, but now that I saw her closer I could see that she was well into her twenties, if not thirty. She stuffed the biscuits into her mouth.

'Any cake?' she asked Molly. She looked at me and her green cat's eyes narrowed. 'What you doin' here anyways? Who asked you to come?' She spoke in a rough accent.

Her sudden aggression took me aback. 'I'm writing a book,' I said. 'About a man called Wadhurst Carpenter.' My voice came out thin and not quite in control. I took a deep breath and spoke again. 'Cecil Durrant comes into it.'

'Go back where you came from,' Jenny said. 'Get out of here while you can, there's nothing here for you.' She sounded matter-of-fact, not hostile any more, but certainly not friendly. I felt intimidated, amazed. Jenny glared at me with those marvellous greenish eyes.

Molly put a cup of tea on the table and pushed a plate with a slice of fruit cake towards her. There was a pause.

'Don't say I didn't warn you,' Jenny said, then she grabbed the piece of cake and rushed out of the kitchen, jerking the table as she went so the tea spilled out of the cup.

I didn't know what to say.

Molly wrung out a cloth and wiped the table where Jenny had spilled the tea. 'Sure, you mustn't mind Jenny,' she said, 'there's no harm in her.'

But I'd been startled and now I was angry. 'I've never heard anything like it,' I said. 'What made her behave like that? Is she mad?'

'Oh, no, nothing of that sort,' Molly said, 'that's her way with strangers. She's quite worldly-wise, our Jenny, and she knows the Durrants aren't. She's afraid strangers might abuse that about them. She's very attached to Miss Hilda, that's the truth. She likes to protect her.'

It hadn't sounded like that to me. It had sounded like a warning to me that I might be in danger. But I said, 'If Hilda isn't mad why should Jenny think she has to protect her from me? What does she think I'm going to do, steal the vegetables out of her garden? She takes a lot on herself, it seems to me, insulting a guest of the Durrants like that. I've seen her skulking round in the garden, I've a good mind to say something to Hilda. What's her job here, anyway?'

'Oh, no,' Molly said, 'you don't understand. She doesn't work here, she's family. Jenny is Miss Hilda's daughter.'

ten

I was profoundly shocked by Molly's revelation about Jenny. In spite of being an Oxford graduate and a child of the Permissive Society, I couldn't conceive of Hilda having anything to do with sex. But I could imagine how devastating Hilda's pregnancy must have been for the Durrants in the 1930s.

I sat at Cecil Durrant's desk and tried to guess what the old man must have felt when Hilda broke the news and told him she was expecting. I was surprised it didn't kill him on the spot. I put away the older diaries and skipped a decade or so to try to find a mention of Hilda's bombshell, but without success. I stared out of the window as he probably did that day, long ago. The wind was flattening the unmown grass on the lawn so it looked like a sheet of water. The bamboo canes sounded like cracking whips and there was rain hurling itself against the glass. And then, as always, there was the sound of the sea crashing against the rocks, but multiplied by gale force ten.

I wondered, Did Hilda tell her mother first? But one look at the flinty eyes and tightly folded little mouth of that portrait of Caroline Durrant on the study wall, and I knew that in her position I could never tell a mother like that.

'Darling Mummum' would have had Hilda locked up for life in a lunatic asylum without a qualm. Morally insane they called it in those days. That poor girl, what must it have been like for her? And then there was the big question – who was the father? Was Cecil Durrant eccentric enough to believe in immaculate conception? Would he have blamed Hilda, or detest the man who had abused his darling daughter? She couldn't have known what was happening. She was abnormally innocent now, she must have been positively emotionally retarded then. What kind of man would have taken advantage of someone like that? That was what I kept asking myself, and I could find only one answer to all my questions.

The only person I could think of as Jenny's father was Wadhurst Carpenter.

I kept telling myself it was out of the question. Why would such a man have bothered with Hilda Durrant? And he was a gentleman. He'd known her as a child. She was the daughter of his mentor and friend, and, on a lower level, he wouldn't risk the professional scandal. But if such considerations didn't stand in his way, Wadhurst Carpenter wouldn't have left Hilda in the lurch, he'd have married her. Even so, he seemed to be the only man aged under fifty within miles of Balcurran House. But he didn't have any contact with Patience or Hilda. I'd asked Hilda about him once, and she said she'd never known him because he was considered a moral danger to young women and Cecil Durrant kept him out of the way of his daughters.

I didn't want to think of Wadhurst Carpenter in the role of Hilda's lover or Jenny's father. I was jealous. He was *my* hero. My mind was filled with thoughts of him. There was nothing wrong with that, after all, I was at Balcurran House for just that purpose. If Wadhurst Carpenter had loved Hilda Durrant, so be it. But I didn't believe it. There had to be someone else.

eleven

I remember quite clearly how I felt. I was embarrassed and a little nostalgic recalling the confused emotions of my own much younger self. I felt sad for that former me. All that overheated passion, it was more than hero worship for the object of my study. Clearly that raw, over-protected, not particularly attractive, student I was in 1966 was falling in love with a mythic Wadhurst Carpenter. It wasn't so surprising, given how naive I was then. I was like a girl obsessed by a poster of a film star.

Indeed, everything to do with what was happening to me at Balcurran House buffeted my awakening senses one way or another – the smell of sea on the wind, the sharp tang of peat fires, the feel of the tooled leather as I opened a new volume of Cecil Durrant's diaries. And though nothing had really been happening to me at Balcurran House, I was full of expectation that it might, and if it did, I couldn't predict what it would be. That's what it means to be young, I suppose. Anticipation consumed me like a fever. I laughed too much, I burst into tears for no good reason, I had to wind my legs around the dining room chair at mealtimes to keep them still. Later on it would cause me much distress, but I don't think I even noticed at that point that Alison did not reply to my letters. Or, at least, I didn't care. Writing to her gave me an outlet for the intensity of my feelings. I didn't really want a reply. Anything she'd said in reply would have bludgeoned my happy illusion with tough reality. Simply, it was writing about Wadhurst Carpenter to an outsider like Alison which made him more real to me. It was a form of virtual consummation.

Of course, all this pent-up emotion must have coloured the way I interpreted what the Cecil Durrant diaries were revealing about the young Hilda. I see so clearly now how I channelled all that emotion. Reading these fragments from the past makes me think that Cecil Durrant had a point about fact and fiction. We make up our own emotions and they are not the truth. I'd wanted the truth about Jenny, though. Even then, I was enough of an embryonic historical biographer to know I had to find it.

So how did I set about it? As far as I remember, I took the obvious way to check my facts. I returned to the kitchen where Molly was bent over the sink, scrubbing baking sheets with wire wool. She looked up as I came in. 'Sure, I expected you'd be back to hear the truth of it,' she said. 'You looked as if you'd seen a ghost.'

I laughed. 'You certainly got me that time,' I said. 'You had me believing it was true. Come to that, I still don't know what to believe. It isn't true, is it?'

Molly stacked the last baking tray on the draining board and took a towel to dry her hands. I followed the old woman's gaze out of the window and we both watched the Burne-Jones' Jenny come out of one of the stone buildings into the courtyard, dragging a half-empty feed sack across the cobbles in a decidedly un-Pre-Raphaelite scene.

'Poor child,' Molly said, almost under her breath, 'it hasn't brought her much happiness for herself, sure it hasn't.'

'What happened?' I found myself whispering, as though I were asking Molly to enter forbidden territory. 'She's not really Hilda's daughter, is she?'

'Oh, aye, that she is, signed and sealed.' Then Molly must have decided that she'd had enough fun teasing me. 'She's legally adopted,' she said. 'It was a family they wanted. Miss Patience was to have a boy and Miss Hilda a girl, but there never was a boy, just poor little Jenny. They adopted her, the two of them did, God help them. Never said nothing about it, one day they went to the orphanage and brought her back with them like a stray kitten.'

I was astonished. 'But why?' I asked.

'Sure, wasn't she one of their good works?' Molly said. She sounded sad, as though she could have told them, if they'd asked her, that good works never did anyone any good. 'Weren't they full of good works? The house was always full of animals and birds they were looking after. Miss Hilda more than Miss Patience, but then Miss Hilda was always shy and kept away from people, so it was she liked to look after the animals more. Until the Master was ill, that is, then she nursed him as though her life depended on it. They all helped, but she did more than anyone, with him day and night she was, God love her. She went down to a shadow, going without meals, sitting up at night when he was restless.'

'What happened to the animals then?' The question slipped out and I wished I hadn't spoken. I was thinking of Molly's childhood and the incident of Hilda and the injured bird, but Molly seemed not to have heard me. She went on with her story.

'After the Master died, didn't she look after the Mistress

then who was so upset? I've never seen anything like it. She took to her bed for days, Mrs Durrant did, we could hear her weeping from the kitchen here, through stone walls and the staircase, as though her heart was broken. It wasn't natural. She never cried, she disapproved of crying, but she cried then.'

Molly now seemed to remember my question. 'The animals were dead by then,' she said. 'The animals always died. They were wild things, they died of fear.'

I had a sudden, horrible intuition of the suffering of a wild creature held captive in the house, so frightened that it died of it. The warm kitchen seemed suddenly a chilling place.

Molly Dunn said, 'There was nothing left for Miss Hilda to look after then.'

'So they decided to adopt a child?' I knew I sounded disbelieving. I couldn't help it.

'They did so.' Molly's tone held a hint of defiance. 'They adopted Jenny. Her name was Janet, on the register, but they called her Jenny because Miss Hilda said she was a little bright bird who hopped into the house, their Jenny Wren. How Miss Hilda loved her, right from the start. I'll never forget the way she looked at her when they brought her into the house. She took her out of Miss Patience's arms and took her away there and then to the nursery she'd made ready.'

Once again I was filled with the fear of a wounded wild animal wrapped in an old blanket in a place which held more terrors by far than the cold earth. 'What about Patience?' I said.

'She had her own plans. She wanted Jenny to be the best Durrant they could make her, for her own good. There's a lot of her mother in Miss Patience.'

'Who was she, this Jenny? Did they know anything about her?'

Molly bent over the sink and spoke over her shoulder as though, if she didn't look directly at me, she could not be accused of telling me something the Durrants might not want me to know. ''Twas thought that her mother was Kathleen, a kitchen maid in the Master's time,' Molly said, muttering. 'That's how the story went then.'

'She was here at Balcurran House?'

'She was sent away in disgrace. The Master turned her out of the house.'

'Why? What did she do?'

Molly turned back to face me. She could not resist the reflected excitement of telling the old scandal. 'I can't say for certain. There were stories. There was a fire started deliberately in the night and one of the kitchen servants had to go to hospital.'

'And later on you think this Kathleen was Jenny's mother? Did the Durrants know that when they adopted her?'

Molly stood looking out of the window into the courtyard. I saw from the faraway look in her eyes that she was trying to recapture the scene from that past era. 'Kathleen came back,' she said, 'it must have been a month or so before the Master died. She wanted work. Miss Hilda found her outside the back door one day in a right state of it, half-starved. I remember that day like it was yesterday, I'd never seen Miss Hilda so excited as she was then with another waif to care for. She brought Kathleen into the kitchen to me and sat her down at the table.'

Molly shivered suddenly and crossed herself. 'I can see her now,' she said. 'God help her, scrawny little thing, dirty she was, her clothes in rags, with her hair all wet and caked so it looked like dried blood. Miss Hilda said, "Isn't she a poor little thing, Molly, we must feed her up and look after her." I could see at once what her condition was, though I didn't know how near she was to her time.'

'Did Hilda know?'

'Know?'

'I mean, did Miss Hilda know that Kathleen was going to have a baby?'

'Bless you, she'd never think of such a thing. But Mrs Durrant heard the girl crying and she came in and she knew at once. I saw the look on her face, and then she sent Miss Hilda out on some errand and started to ask Kathleen how far gone she was and where was the father.'

'Did Kathleen say who the father was?'

'I had to go and find her something to eat. When I came back Mrs Durrant said the girl had some tale about tinkers who'd been working on the turf-cutting down Connemara way and she'd gone with them when they moved on. She and one of the lads were going to look for work up the coast, but when she told him about the baby he left her and she never saw him again.'

'Poor Kathleen,' I said.

'Be that as it may,' Molly said, 'she'd a nerve coming back here after what had happened. Mrs Durrant said to me "Molly, we must have her out of here by the time Miss Hilda gets back", and then she went to get her purse.'

'Why?' I asked. 'Why was she in such a hurry to get rid of her before Hilda came back?'

Molly was impatient with me, as though I was being deliberately stupid. 'Miss Hilda was prone to notions,' she said. 'I think there was a fear that Miss Hilda would have taken the girl under her wing and kept her here. She'd have been one of Miss Hilda's poor victims, hidden away and looked after. Kathleen, who was a scheming little minx, thought she knew things about Miss Hilda, you see, she thought she knew things Mrs Durrant would never want known. Some people round here thought Miss Hilda wasn't sane, you know? The family said she was over-sensitive. Mrs Durrant was very angry with Kathleen for coming here and starting all that up again, though like as not that's why Kathleen came. Blackmail is a harsh word, to be sure, but anyway, she'd have been sure Miss Hilda would look after her. But Mrs Durrant gave her some money and told her to leave at once or she'd have her thrown out.'

'And Kathleen went?'

'Oh, yes. She'd got what she came for, food and money.'

'What did Hilda say when she found Kathleen had gone?'

'Oh, she was all for going after the girl and bringing her back and keeping her there in her room in secret, like another of those animals and birds she looked after, that's all I meant,' Molly said. I could tell from her tone that Molly was wondering whether she should go on with her story.

'What happened then?' I prompted her. For a moment I thought that Molly wouldn't answer, but at last she went on.

'Well, as I remember it Miss Patience came in then and Mrs Durrant told her about Kathleen and Miss Patience went very white and she said to Miss Hilda that she was on her way to Porterstown to visit in the hospital and she said she would pick up Kathleen on the road and take her to a place where she'd be looked after in the town.'

'What kind of place did she mean? Was there somewhere she'd be looked after then?'

'I don't know, I'm sure, where she took the girl, but Miss Patience knew that kind of thing, she did a lot of voluntary work in those days, and she must've done something because the next we knew was months after when she and

Miss Hilda went to an orphanage in Galway town and brought Jenny home with them for good. I don't know how she managed that because Kathleen was a Catholic girl and the Church wouldn't like a pair of Protestant women bringing up a child out of its religion.'

I began absent-mindedly to stack the baking trays that Molly had left to drain. 'What did they expect to get out of it, bringing up a baby like that?' I wondered aloud.

'That wasn't the way of it at all,' Molly said, 'it wasn't something they wanted for themselves, it was their duty. They knew by then they wouldn't have children of their own. Miss Hilda may have wanted to look after her as though she was injured, like the animals, and in a way she was, wasn't she, with the damage done to her by the circumstances of her birth? But mostly they wanted to bring her up as a Durrant, a real Durrant.'

'But—'

'I know, how could they expect to do that? But they gave her everything,' Molly said. She spoke in a firm voice, allowing no questioning of what she said. 'She had everything money could buy.'

'But the Durrants weren't rich, were they? It must have been difficult to make ends meet after Mr Durrant died. I know his friend Wadhurst Carpenter got some kind of official pension for the old man, but that probably stopped when he died. How did they support a child?'

'Sure, didn't they have to earn the money themselves, what else could they do? That's when Miss Patience started her work collecting all those seeds and crossing one specimen of a flower with another and writing up her notes on her experimentations for the scientific magazines and the professors in Dublin at Trinity College, and Miss Hilda took up commissions for her paintings of flowers and insects and the like. They did it all for the child, for Jenny. They were like different people. They were as good as mother and father to that child. She had nothing but the best, they sent her to an expensive boarding school in England.'

'They did?' I couldn't connect the rude and dirty girl I'd seen with that sort of education.

Molly lowered her voice until she was almost whispering. 'She went to school in England with little girls with titles as long as your arm, and she was taught to play the piano and sing and she had dancing lessons, and deportment and elocution. Can you credit that?'

This vision of feminine refinement seemed so far removed from the rough-voiced Jenny whom I could still see looking like a scarecrow across the yard that I couldn't help smiling. 'I thought she was a local girl who came to help out,' I said. 'Her accent's so broad....'

'And isn't that Jenny for you?' Molly sighed, then got up and started to put tea things on a silver tray with what looked like a low wooden fence around its edge. 'Doesn't she do it to tease? They did everything they could to make her into a real young Miss Durrant,' she said, 'but they never asked her what she thought about it. Our Jenny had other ideas.' Molly laughed at the memory. 'She wouldn't take her meals with them, or sit with them in the evenings, or do anything at all with them. Still won't. You'd think she hated them. She did hate Mrs Durrant, I grant you that, she really did, and then Miss Patience too, she never was close to her. Miss Hilda's the one she loved, but of course Miss Hilda was always with the family, Jenny could never get her to herself. So Jenny gave up loving Miss Hilda as a bad job in the end, she looked elsewhere to get the attention she wanted. And of course once she didn't care even what Miss Hilda thought of her, she did what she liked. The moment she was home from school on her holidays she'd be away with the village girls, smoking and drinking and goodness knows what else, there were boys there too, not just girls. I dread to think what Miss Patience would have done to her if she'd known. Jenny used to come back here most nights staggering with drink and her clothes all anyhow, and her only fourteen or fifteen.'

There was a short silence before Molly added: 'Sure, I know what you're thinking, and don't think I haven't thought the same myself. Blood will out. That child never knew her mother or father; she came here at a few weeks old and she never knew anything but the life of a real lady, and yet when she came back here on her school holidays, it was us she came to see here in the kitchen and it was as though she was one of us, the way she was, a right little gurrier.'

I didn't know the word, but I got its meaning from the way she said it.

'What did the Durrants think about that?' I asked.

'They just went on treating her as though it wasn't happening. They gave her a pony, but she wasn't interested. They did everything they could to show they loved her.'

'Did they really,' I asked, 'love her? Or did they just think they ought to? It sounds as though she made it difficult.'

I could imagine the kind of nightmare it must have been for the Durrants. Jenny must have seemed like a monster to them, so completely different from anything they'd ever experienced themselves. They were probably terrified for her, or did I mean terrified *of* her? I put the thought firmly aside. I didn't want to think of Jenny's kind of terrorism.

Molly had begun to answer the question I'd asked about the Durrants' love for Jenny. 'Oh, they loved her all right,' she said. 'She was family, as far as they were concerned. They thought it was their fault if she wasn't happy. And, God love them, they couldn't understand why she wasn't happy. But it would never have occurred to them not to love her. She had the family name. That was part of it, and they knew she needed them. That was always the way to the hearts of Miss Patience and Miss Hilda.'

'She must've made them unhappy though.'

'Oh, no, she didn't, she made them happy. It made them happy to have her. They never doubted that they could change her, that they could train her to be a real Durrant. Miss Hilda used to say when she came down here looking for her, "Love will prevail, Molly".'

I wondered if she was making this up. I couldn't see Hilda saying anything so intimate to Molly. 'But it hasn't prevailed, has it?' I said. 'She hates everything about them.' As soon as I said this I thought that perhaps I'd gone too far. 'She seems to have as little to do with them as she can,' I added.

'Yes.' Molly's voice was thoughtful. 'That's how it looks, of course. But then, perhaps, as they say, you shouldn't judge by appearances.'

I didn't argue with her. I thought she didn't understand Jenny, how could she? There was no confusion in Molly's life; she was what she was born to be. She'd wanted nothing else.

But I did ask one more question. 'Molly, what happened to Kathleen?'

She shook her head as though repudiating the question. 'We'll never know,' she said.

twelve

What did that mean, we'll never know? I confided my speculations to Alison.

Dear Alison,

What do you think of this for a theory? How about Cecil Durrant as Jenny's natural father? It would be quite natural then that Hilda and Patience should adopt the baby. It makes sense of all that stuff about making her into a true Durrant. She was one. If Cecil Durrant were the child's father, it would explain why the Catholic orphanage gave the baby to Protestants to raise.

Of course the Durrants would want to keep it quiet. Mrs Durrant must've known, though. Perhaps that's why the old lady was so angry with Kathleen. It explains why Jenny hated Mrs Durrant so much, too. Even Molly Dunn admits she hated her. You've only got to see her picture to know she'd make any love child of her husband's suffer. And Jenny's got red hair, like Cecil Durrant. Oh, yes, so had Kathleen. It's mentioned in one of the diaries. But Cecil Durrant must have noticed her to bother mentioning it. She was very pretty, according to Molly Dunn.

I know what you're going to say, and I admit it's a big stumbling block. But old men can be predatory about young girls. But no, I suppose it's not really possible. Jenny was born after Cecil Durrant died, and he was ill for months before that. It's a pity the facts always seem to stand in the way of a romantic story, but I've got to stick to what I can prove if I'm ever going to get to the truth. I'm sorry, I'm sure you'd much rather have the fantastical version to keep you amused while your poor leg mends.

By the way, when you write back – or should that be if, given the lack of response from you so far – don't mention any of what I've said in this letter. Someone might see your reply, and if by chance the Durrants suspected what I've told you, they'd probably lock me up and throw away the key.

My work on Wadhurst Carpenter goes well. I found a letter from him which may lead to something promising. It's only a page of something much longer, so I can't tell who he's writing to. Obviously he never posted it, anyway, but it mentions how he's been making notes on Patience and Hilda because he's interested in a study of the importance of environment in the upbringing of middle-class British girls compared with young women in Arabia. Did he think Cecil Durrant was like a tyrannical Arab father controlling his daughters? But then, in those countries, all the training is designed to make girls into obedient sex objects put on earth to satisfy their husbands and have sons. Whereas the Durrant girls were kept in ignorance. Boy, would I like to find those notes! I wonder if Cecil Durrant found out what Wadhurst Carpenter was doing? I should think that would've been enough to get him banished from Balcurran House for ever.

thirteen

13 April 1934:
Sir George Gilroy and his mother here to tea and to look at the garden, which is now coming to life after the long winter and a wet month of March. Sir George's mother is a formidable woman of fearsome aspect. Conversation did not flow easily once the garden was exhausted as a source of interest. The termagant fired a look of disapproval at our little red-haired maid Kathleen, a clumsy maiden enough, which perhaps was her offence, and the poor child was so overcome that she dropped a cup and plate, then fled from the scene in tears. Dear Mummum promised the Gilroy woman that she would have a word with the girl about her behaviour, which has been erratic of late. The incident, however, happily launched Sir George's mother on the subject of servants and conversation no longer flagged, a case of an ill wind....

24 April 1934:
There is no room for doubt, according to the report of the firemen who attended on us. Our worst fears are true. The fire which has caused such damage here was

no accidental blaze, it was lighted deliberately. We sat together, dear Mummum and myself, Patience and my Hildina, in the drawing room, which has happily been spared from damage except for the residue of smoke stains and the smell of ash, and we tried to look into our hearts to see who might have a grudge of such degree against us that they would try deliberately to destroy our home and our lives. We have removed ourselves from the world, we take no part in politics. Simply, we do not know who started the fire but together we said a prayer and asked God to forgive them, as we do. It is a fearful thing to have to watch on one's children's faces, the realization that there could be people in the world who, with no reason, do not necessarily wish them well.

27 April 1934:

We are all deeply disturbed by what has happened in this house. It is something unlooked for in our happy home, but there is no hiding our knowledge now. It must be bravely faced by us all. Dear Mummum has borne the greatest burden. She it was who reached the truth of the matter. She had cause to question the girl Kathleen about the fire. Kathleen, a poor simple girl with neither wit nor industry, agreed amid a burst of weeping that she had indeed laid and lighted the blaze. It seems she took this wicked course in the heat of passion for a youth whom dear Mummum in her innocence had taken on to help with the gardening over the summer. This young man had given Kathleen to understand that he loved her and would marry her. But she then discovered her faithless swain in the embrace of another. Hence, poor demented creature, in order to express her anger at this man's betrayal, she set fire to the house and caused the blaze which threatened us all. So be it, God's will be done.

fourteen

So, Jenny's mother was an arsonist, perhaps even a would-be murderess. I wasn't surprised, there was a savage quality about Jenny that was quite scary.

Anyway, there was something that happened that spooked me. If it weren't for being so wrapped up in finding Wadhurst Carpenter's note on the Durrant daughters, I think I would have got out of there. But I couldn't face having to go back to Newcastle without achieving anything. This begged the question of how I would escape, anyway. I had no money, and no way of getting any unless Hilda took me to Porterstown, which she was still blithely managing to put off doing.

I was in my room because I couldn't face returning to the study to read more of Cecil Durrant's script. His writing was like purl knitting, and, I felt too restless to decipher it. The house was incredibly oppressive. This might have been all right for Alison's tastes in fiction, but in real life it got me down. It was probably just my imagination, but I couldn't explain the undercurrent of menace in Balcurran House among those people. I had been feeling like this for days.

The evenings were closing in and even at 4.30 the sun had almost sunk, if there was any sun, that is. Usually it just got dark. The skies were fantastic there, and when there was a sunset it was a blaze of wild intense colour which looked like an enormous black opal, like the one of Hilda's brooch. I think she'd have liked that conceit, her jewel being a chip off the evening sky.

I left the house through the french windows in the drawing room – the musty one which the family didn't use with wisteria practically covering the entire window. I wanted to be alone. I knew that Patience would be working for another two hours and she wouldn't see me from her office above the courtyard. Actually, even if she was staring out of the window I didn't think she'd see me. I couldn't think why she didn't admit her sight was gone. Maybe the doctors could do something. But I couldn't say anything about it. Everyone behaved as though everything was normal. Anyway, Patience was working, but I wasn't sure where Hilda was and I didn't want her to see me. Frankly, a stately promenade around the lawn with Hilda with the yapping dogs was the last thing I needed.

Once I'd escaped, I stopped and looked back at the house, and I must say that whoever built it must have been mad, or else he'd never grown out of a fascination with Grimm's fairytales, adding gables and turrets and balustrades which seemed to bear no relation to the rooms as they were inside. And then there was wisteria crawling over the walls with boughs all knotted and twisted. I suppose the place might have been impressive if it had all been built in the pale stone of the front porch, but the rest was a particularly harsh shade of dark-red brick which seems to have nothing to do with the bleak rocky landscape round here.

I stood there looking at it, thinking how ugly the place was, and it seemed to me that whoever designed it could not have had a loving heart. In this setting it looked like an archi-tectural experiment, part residence, part trophy, to be lived in by human guinea pigs.

On one side the sea glinted in the sun. I had to put my hand up to shield my eyes, but it was still too bright to look at. That was why I went round the side of the house to escape the glare. I found a damp path smelling of mouldy wet leaves, which led into a dark tunnel of rhododendron and laurel. I felt far away from the ordinary world. I had a kind of superstitious fear of Balcurran House which I didn't understand. Perhaps that was why I kept writing to Alison, in the hope that getting it down on paper might have cleared my mind. And every morning I expected a letter when Molly brought the post with her when she came, but there was nothing.

Anyway, my footsteps were muffled by the leaf mould on the path. The sharp tang of damp earth smelt of disillusion. It was quite silent among the dark, twisted branches of the rhododendrons. Somewhere ahead a blackbird screamed an alarm call, but that was all. Then the path came out of the tunnel of overgrown shrubbery into a grass-covered clearing. In the middle was a small stone building with a single window roughly boarded up and a heavy hobnailed door which stood ajar. The light had gone out of the sky by now and the outlines of the shack were blurred in the shadow of the trees. I had a very strong feeling that I was interrupting something, though there wasn't any sign of life that I could see.

I called out, 'Hullo, is anyone there?'

The grass was already damp with dew, but I didn't notice my feet were wet as I went over and pushed the door. It creaked, then swung open.

I was inside an old well-house. There was a circular brick parapet in the middle around the edge of the shaft. The wooden cover had half-rotted away. I could see where there used to be a heavy iron pump with a handle fitted at one side, but this was now askew. I lifted the pump handle and a flake of rusted metal fell off. I heard the splash as it hit water, echoing faintly from a very, very long way down. The place seemed as if no one had been there for years. But then as my eyes got used to the gloom I saw that someone had been there recently. There was a pile of rags under the boarded window. I went across and pulled at one. They were blankets; and they didn't feel damp at all. There was a sleeping bag, too, neatly folded against the wall. I backed away and as I did there was a terrible clatter as I knocked over a storm lantern on the floor. The atmosphere of Balcurran House and the Durrant sisters had got so much on my nerves that I ran out of there in terror, pulling the door shut behind me. Outside it was almost dark. At the far side of the glade I stopped and took several deep breaths, trying to calm the stupid thumping of my heart.

That's when I thought I saw a dark figure of a man break away from the silhouette of a tree trunk and flit across the edge of the clearing. Then he disappeared behind the building. I heard the sound of a breaking branch, then nothing. I was petrified. I fled across the clearing back into the dark tunnel of rhododendron and laurel towards the house. I shot out of the shrubbery onto the open lawn and stopped in front of the house, and then I felt ridiculous. The back of my neck prickled with sweat and I was breathing like a grampus in the cold air. I looked back into the dense darkness of the rhododendrons and laurels. There was nothing there at all. Even the birds weren't moving.

What had got into me? It was panic, real panic in the ancient Greek sense. But did I really see a man by the well-house? Or was it a tree stirred by a gust of wind? And if it was a man, why did I panic? He was probably some harmless tramp using the building as shelter. I'm sure I over-reacted anyway, if there was a man he wasn't doing any harm, there was no need to be hysterical. But I knew all that, and I was still petrified. I wondered if I should say anything to the Durrants. They wouldn't like having a strange man sheltering in their well-house. They'd probably have him locked up, accuse him of planning to rob them. Perhaps he *was* planning to rob them, in which case there was a good chance that he'd get as far away from the well-house as possible once he knew I had seen him. I wondered how Patience and Hilda would react to my story.

They might laugh at me for having an overactive imagination. Or they might be terrified if they thought there had been a strange man around. There had been a time in the history of this house when a fleeting glimpse of a strange man in the bushes could mean the firing of the building, or a Fenian assassin. However deep that fear of strange men was buried in the past, it was still a subconscious reality in the minds of women like Patience and Hilda. For them a strange man was a thing of real deep-rooted terror. Hilda was paranoid enough already, she might go right off her head, and probably for nothing at all. It was almost dark and with all those trees, the eyes play tricks. I most likely imagined the whole thing and there wasn't any man. That was most likely. Balcurran House was spooky enough at the best of times, it was best to forget the whole thing.

But I couldn't get it out of my mind. Hilda asked me at supper how I was getting on with my research and I wasn't thinking and started to blurt out about Wadhurst

Carpenter's note about Cecil Durrant's parenting skills. That was the last thing I wanted her to know, and it certainly wasn't something she wanted to hear. I managed to change tack just in time and I found myself telling her how I couldn't concentrate on specific mentions of Wadhurst Carpenter because I got so carried away by the interesting things her father said about their family life. That wasn't exactly what I wanted her to know either! Patience became instantly suspicious and said something like, 'Really? I thought we always lived such a quiet and uneventful life, didn't you, Hilda?' She did her thing – snapping her mouth shut with that little smile, but I couldn't let her change the subject now.

I tried to find words that wouldn't offend them or seem prurient, so I said, 'It's the way he writes about himself and your mother and everyone here, he makes them come alive as people. It's a pity he wasn't a writer, he's really great.'

'That's curious,' Patience said, 'because I don't think he was particularly interested in people.'

Hilda was indignant about that. 'Patience, of course he was. That's a terrible thing to say about anyone. He loved people. I've never known a man so full of love and understanding for people, you know he was.'

'I'm not saying he wasn't,' Patience said, 'that's not what I meant. But I believe he was more interested in their thoughts and ideas than he was in their everyday doings and feelings. He didn't understand such things. He had no time to waste on people who weren't capable of rational thought. I was merely surprised that Frances should find the musings of such a philosopher so diverting.'

Hilda turned to me as though apologizing for misjudging me. 'You sound as though you were *enjoying* his writings,' she said, 'it doesn't really seem like work, does it?'

No doubt about it, I wouldn't rate as one of Cecil Durrant's chosen few, not as far as Hilda Durrant was concerned. She was definitely beginning to think of me as a time-waster. Anyway, I tried to make out that it wasn't as if I was interested in *gossip*, but of course that was exactly what I was interested in, so I had to pretend to swallow something the wrong way because I blush when I lie.

'We were a close family, that's all,' Hilda said. 'I think all close families are similar. What about your own family, dear? I expect you're close?'

And I said yes, we were and then I had to pretend to cough again because that was a lie too. Of course I didn't have anything to hide but I didn't think Hilda wanted to hear my theories about family life forcing people into moulds they don't fit, it might turn her against me. I could never make the daughters of Cecil Durrant as revealed in his diaries understand that. As far as they were concerned, family life was *the* source of strength and privilege in society that they would never question its corporate identity.

I changed the subject. I asked straight out who Jenny was.

Patience said, 'But I thought you met her the night you arrived?' She did sound a bit upset, but not as though a secret had been betrayed, more as though there had been a breach of good manners.

'Jenny is our daughter,' Hilda said. 'We adopted her as a darling little baby after Father died.'

'But why—?'

Patience said, 'Why did we adopt her, or why doesn't she eat with us, and sit with us in the evenings? Is that what you want to know?' I could hear her lips snap together, and then her tone was so cold it was like an easterly wind in the room. I definitely felt they were closing ranks. Patience was smiling with a slightly patronizing air, as though she under-stood that I must be curious, but felt it was a lapse of manners to show it.

'Jenny is a young woman,' Hilda said. 'She has better things to do than spend her time with two old women like us.'

'But she lives here?'

'Of course. Didn't she open the door to you when you first came? She has her own little place at the back, she did it up for herself. She worked so hard, and she's so proud of it.' Hilda in turn looked proud, as though she'd achieved some-thing herself. 'She likes to look after her home and cook for herself, she prefers a less formal life than we're used to.'

'Does she have a job? I mean, a career sort of job?' It was a silly question, of course. I knew she didn't. What kind of career could she have in a desolate part of the world like this? What kind of career could Jenny have anywhere, come to think of it? But I wanted to find out more and even a silly question was better than the dumb-founded silence I'd have been reduced to otherwise.

Hilda suddenly pushed back her chair and stood up, saying, 'You must ask her yourself. I'll fetch her.'

She went out and I couldn't think of anything to say to make conversation with Patience. In the end she said, 'Maybe she can help you in your work. Jenny is very clever, you know, she did very well at school. Her teachers hoped that she would go on to university. But she wasn't interested. She preferred to come home.' It was disconcerting how she seemed to face me directly but be looking past me at someone else I didn't know was in the room.

'It was a brave thing for you and Hilda to do,' I said.

'Brave?' Patience was laughing, the way people laugh

when there's no real reason for it but they don't know what else to do. She obviously thought I was being particularly dense. 'You mean adopting her? No, it wasn't brave. We are very fortunate, Hilda and I, we had a wonderful loving family, a life of privilege. After Father died, we decided that by then we would not get married and have children of our own. We wanted to involve ourselves with someone young to carry us – the Durrant family – on into the future. I suppose you young persons would say we wanted to put our imprint on the future, even a small imprint.'

'But surely,' I said, 'that's simply the genetic imperative, it can't apply to you two and Jenny, she's not blood.'

I thought I might have gone a bit too far, but she ignored me and went on, 'We felt we owed it to … well, to life, I suppose, or God or whatever you like to call it, to our parents, to share what we have with a poor child who had no such advantages.'

'You mean if a Durrant wasn't going to be born, you'd make one? What an experiment!' I was angry, more so because I didn't know why. Anyway, I was sure I had gone too far this time.

'An experiment?' Patience said. She was horrified. 'Oh, no,' she said, 'not an experiment. You make it sound so crude, as though we wanted to turn Jenny into something she wasn't. It wasn't like that at all. We wanted her to be herself, no one else, but the best she could be if there was nothing in her way to stop her. That's how she would be a Durrant. A child reflects the love she receives wherever it comes from, don't you think?'

'But how can you be sure what she'd turn out to be, when you don't know where she comes from? She could just be a better criminal.'

'Don't you think that if a child is happy, she will be good. It's the law of Nature.'

That kind of goodness seemed to me positively sinister. Anyway, I couldn't let her get away with it, so I said, 'What happens if a child is happy when she's bad?'

'Oh, my dear, how can she be? Even in the warped circumstances you're suggesting, if the child is loved, she is happy and will be good in order to continue to be loved. If she is bad, it is because she is not loved enough. Don't you believe that?'

'No,' I said, 'I believe love like that is the most destructive force in the world.' I didn't know if I really meant that. Or, indeed, what I really meant by it. Anyway, there was a long silence.

Then Patience said, very quietly, 'Until we had the gift of Jenny, our lives were ... well, passive. Oh, we tried to help others, Mother was famous for her charity work, and I used to help out at the TB hospital in Porterstown. And Hilda was always looking after animals and birds. But Jenny opened our hearts to the joys of real work with a purpose.'

'Aren't good works an end in themselves?'

'I mean something more. Work as part of creation, creating a family to take over the future.'

I couldn't argue, so I changed the subject and said something obvious like, 'I know babies are very demanding.' They must have been well into middle age when Jenny arrived and even natural mothers near forty find a first baby tough going.

But she wasn't to be deflected. She said, 'No, not that. We had to start earning our living, to keep her. We had to start making use of the talents God gave us. She turned us into doers, not takers. I'd done a fair bit of gardening and I started gathering seeds and cross-germinating plants to create new strains, and I found there was a market for them. It went on from there. Thank God I was doing well by the time we had to find school fees.'

'And Hilda?'

'Hilda was not able to go out to work, she was vulnerable and she had to be here with the baby. But, you see, God helps those who help themselves. She had always done sketches of flowers and trees, and one of my clients saw some of her work when I sent him a drawing of hers to demonstrate a discovery I'd made. He had a friend who was a publisher and was looking for someone to illustrate a technical book about native Irish plants. It started from there. You can look Hilda up in a pre-War *Who's Who*, she became quite famous.' She paused with an expression on her face that seemed to pray for me to be enlightened with joy. 'If it hadn't been for Jenny's coming,' she said, 'our lives would have been so much less fulfilled than they have been.'

The door opened then and Hilda came in practically pushing Jenny before her.

'Here's our darling little Jenny,' she said. 'Our own little Jenny Wren.'

Jenny was scowling and looked put out. But she had this white skin which sort of glowed like a pearl and she was really quite beautiful up close and when her hair wasn't blowing all over her face. But she was so sulky and bored, it made her seem quite ugly, like someone pulling faces. And she was extremely rude. She pulled away from Hilda and went to the table, using the serving spoon to eat the leftovers of a trifle we'd had for pudding.

Patience said, 'Frances is writing a book. She's studying Father's papers for her research.'

Jenny ignored me.

'Maybe you'd be interested in helping her,' Patience said. 'You were always good at history at school.'

'I wasn't,' Jenny said in a voice that was rough with the local accent and surely much more pronounced than usual. But it wasn't really funny any more. Jenny might have sounded defiant, but there was despair in her voice. As a child she was obviously forced to do work that was beyond her and she still resented the memory of it. But I don't think the Durrants realized this. Patience asked her to sit down and finish her supper with us.

'No fear,' Jenny said. She licked the last of the trifle off the serving spoon and put it back in the dish before going out.

'Dear Jenny,' Hilda said, her voice soft with affection, 'doesn't she have such funny little ways? She loves to tease.'

That night I wrote all this down for Alison, trying to be funny as well as Gothic.

fifteen

27 April 1934:

I cannot distort the truth. It is not so simple. I now come to the part of this sorry tale which I can scarce think of, let alone put into words on paper, without danger of breaking into tears. This Kathleen, pressed to tell the name of the foul seducer, has named Hildina as the woman she saw in the embrace of her rustic lover.

I hope that never in my life may I come closer to striking a woman.

28 April 1934:

In brief, she did not lie. I cannot write more now.

29 April 1934:

It is hard to see how happiness can ever return to our house. The girl is gone from here, and her coarse lover. Dear Mummum weeps. Dear God, help me find a way to forgive my erring daughter. Give me strength to love the sinner and hate the sin. For the present I cannot speak to her, nor look upon her face. I pray for her.

30 April 1934:

I must shoulder the burden of blame. The weakness of

my beloved girl lies at my door. I had forgot that I myself, untroubled as a young man by the sweet demands of the flesh, was set afire by my beloved Caroline at our first meeting in her father's house on that sun-drenched day in Italy. I was driven to the point of madness, so it is I who has passed on to our Hildina this horrid genetic flaw, and I who have caused the flesh of my flesh to be laid open to temptation. I have taken into our home irregular men such as Wadhurst Carpenter and others who do not live by the laws and duties imposed by God. Wadhurst Carpenter's manuscript, the work of a savage and a heathen, full of primitive passions and undiscipline of mind, has lain within my walls and I have not guarded sufficiently against it. I have allowed my children to go out among strangers to nurse the sick and do their Christian duty among the unworthy, and I have not sufficiently protected them from vice and the works of the Devil.

1 May 1934:
We have at last put a seal on the past unhappy month. The love of God has done His work and I am now ashamed of my own lack of faith that this could be so. Hilda is unsoiled. The 'embrace' that Kathleen saw was no more than the comforting gesture of a loving heart. She found the boy distressed and sought to soothe him as she would a poor little hungry hedgehog or a wounded bird that the cat brought in. She did not, in her blessed innocence, understand that such expression of concern is not possible in society between a young girl of her class and a servant.

I give thanks for the lessons learned, and for my

beloved Patience who, unwitting of what has caused our general devastation beyond the fire, has lighted us through our shadowed valley with her sunshine smile and cheerful nature. Mummum, the better to be safe than sorry, has sent away the gardener and also the stable hand. Hilda is thus justly punished by knowing herself the unwitting cause of their suffering. May she gain strength from this knowledge.

Tonight I am weary and with a sad set of mind I find it hard to struggle against a lack of hope. What a task we undertake in living according to God's laws, both now and in our seed for ever and ever.

sixteen

I had no idea what to make of this, but I wrote to Alison, being particularly amusing about the old man believing Hilda's story about 'comforting' the boy. Then I added:

Still no letter from you? I thought you broke your leg, not your arm. Please write, if only so I know you really are getting my letters. Of course, I know you must be, but I'm getting quite paranoid. I've even wondered if Hilda and Patience are intercepting your replies and stopping me from getting any news of the outside world. Of course they'd only be doing that so I won't be distracted from my work, all from the best possible motives. But try to understand – it's weeks now since I got here and I've not been outside the grounds once. If I suggest it, there's always something else to do, and if I press them at all and suggest I could borrow Molly's bicycle, they make snide remarks about the amount of work I've got to do, and they're surprised I should want to let anything get in the way of my studies, which are, after all, the reason they have me staying with them. Oh, they don't put it that crudely, but the implications are clear enough, so I can't insist without being really rude.

I had nightmares that began about this time that there was something they were hiding from me, like there had been a nuclear explosion and the outside world had been blown to pieces. Then something happened that was a bit of a shaker.

Whatever the weather, I tried to go out walking most days, just to get out of the gloomy house. That day, I went outside before lunch. There was a stiff breeze, the sky was a sort of greenish and I could hear the sea battering the cliffs. The Durrant dogs were wrestling on the lawn beyond the shrubbery, even the little drawing-room Pekinese was play-fighting with the others. I felt as full of life as they did. It all seemed so far from my Gothic imaginings that I decided to go down to the well-house and lay to rest the ghost of the other day.

It looked quite different in the mid-morning light, bathed in sunshine – just quaint, not sinister. I opened the door.

The light fell across a man and a woman making love on the pile of old blankets on the floor.

They were naked. She was astride him, and they were really going at it. And then before I could look away, she came and she kind of melted across his chest. He was making these rasping sounds as though she'd stabbed him. His eyes opened and he shouted out and then he saw me over her shoulder. He pushed her away from him so she rolled over onto her back as he was trying to get up and to hide himself at the same time.

The woman was Jenny. She took no notice of me, just lay there with her eyes closed, her legs splayed, the pale skin on her chest flushed bright pink. It clashed with the orange of all that tangled hair. The man managed to pull on his jeans and grab his shoes and shirt. He pushed past me and rushed out of the well-house. Jenny opened her eyes and looked at me without any sign of surprise. She looked marvellous, like a Titian rather than a Burne-Jones. She must've known I couldn't take my eyes off her. She started to laugh at me for staring. I was horribly embarrassed. I said I was sorry, I'd no idea. She sat up with her hands holding her breasts, and her pink nipples poking through her fingers. Bright rose pink.

'About Charlie?' she said.

'Charlie?' I must have looked puzzled.

'You'd no idea about Charlie?' she said. 'You didn't know he was living here?'

There wasn't a trace of the usual rough, gruff accent in her voice. She said, 'His name's Carlos. He's Spanish. I call him Charlie.'

I said, 'I think I saw him here the other day, in the shrubbery.' It was incredible, we could have been talking about the weather.

'He came over here to get work, but he hasn't got the right papers so he keeps out of people's way,' Jenny said. 'He picks up temporary jobs at the hotels up the coast. In between he comes out here and dosses down in this old place. I told him about it. He comes to see me, too, of course.'

I said something about what if it had been Hilda who walked in on her, and she stood up. She looked like a nymph off a classical frieze. She shook the blanket, folding it and putting it aside with the neatly folded sleeping bag I'd seen on my last visit. Then her expression changed. There was a crazy look on her face. 'Oh,' she said, 'I can do what I like with Hilda. She knows better than to get in my way.'

I asked, 'What do you mean?'

'Haven't you heard about Hilda's little notions yet? No, why should you, come to think of it. They're not going to tell you, are they?'

'What notions? What happened?'

'Oh, most likely nothing. It's just stories that go round about people like them who've lived alone in a place like Balcurran House for donkeys' years.'

'What do they say? Tell me.'

'Oh, there was this story about a woman Hilda kept locked up here. For months.'

'That can't be true. You can't believe that.'

'The people round here like to think the worst. They said Hilda kept the woman here against her will and when she was found she was almost starved to death.'

'How was she found, then?'

'Patience found her.'

'It doesn't sound very likely, does it? Why would Hilda do a thing like that?'

'Hilda likes having things to look after, but it's no good if they get better.' Jenny grinned as though she thought what she was saying was funny. She began to put her clothes on as she said, 'Anyway, it was all hushed up. I don't know what really happened. The maids used to tell me about it when I was a kid. They probably just wanted to scare me. They'd tell me Miss Hilda would put me in the well-house in the dark and keep me prisoner if I didn't do what I was told, and if I was very bad she'd make me eat the live fish out of the tank in the boot-room. You know the way those sort of girls make things up.'

I was startled by this sudden snobbery. Looking at her pulling on her shabby clothes it was hard to imagine her as the daughter of a house with maids to wait on her.

She didn't seem to think anything of it. She opened a cupboard by the window. 'Here,' she said, 'there's some paraffin in the stove. Shall we have something to drink? There's tea or cocoa.'

She put the stove on the rim of the well-housing and then shook the small metal kettle that went with the apparatus. 'I don't know if there's enough water,' she said.

'Can't we get it out of the well?' I asked. 'Water's the one thing there should be plenty of in a well-house.'

'Do you have a death-wish or something?' Jenny said. She leaned over the stove and pulled at a stave of the well-cover. There was a distant hollow splash as more wood fell away and dropped into the water at the bottom of the shaft.

'It's quite rotten,' she said, 'that cover wouldn't stop a spider falling through, what's left of it. It looks as though something's already been through, half of it has broken away. Probably a cat. Anyway, I wouldn't fancy drinking that water, not even boiled.' She looked down into the well and then she said in a very matter-of-fact way, 'My mother killed herself by throwing herself down this well.'

'Your mother did what?' My first thought was that Jenny was making up a macabre story to shock me. I actually wondered if she was quite right in the head. 'You shouldn't make up things like that, Jenny,' I said.

'It's true,' she said in that matter-of-fact voice. 'Hilda found her. No one knows what happened. She'd worked here once, my real mother, and they think she probably came here hoping to see me one more time before she did it. I don't remember anything about it. I was only five years old.'

I didn't know what to say. Jenny was unconcerned. She obviously wasn't going to elaborate, so I asked: 'Did you always know you were adopted?'

She laughed at me. 'Chosen,' she said, 'chosen because I was special, Patience and Hilda always told me that. They didn't tell me about my mother killing herself, though, I found that out for myself later.'

Then the wretched kettle whistled, and Jenny began to fuss with the tea. I tried to steer her back to what she'd been saying. 'Who told you?'

She shrugged, so I asked about Carlos. 'How did you meet him?'

'He came by one day at the beginning of the summer,' she said. 'He climbed over the back wall and came to the house. He wanted a job. I saw him. Patience and Hilda were out of the way, working. I felt sorry for him. He hardly spoke any English.'

'Do you speak Spanish?'

'Not so you'd notice, but we both managed a bit of French. And actions speak louder than words, eh?' She winked, making a crude sexual gesture which the Durrants, I was sure, would not have understood. I was embarrassed myself. I didn't like having my nose rubbed in her sexuality.

'We got ... talking,' she said, 'and after that he came back every now and then and it started from there. I got him temporary farm work along the coast, so he stuck around.'

'How could you help him get work?' I saw Jenny as a sort of permanent prisoner at Balcurran House, without friends or neighbours. How could she have created a secret alternative life, more or less normal, in spite of the rigid bounds of the Durrants' regime? But then I found the whole subject of Jenny fascinating, she was a kind of divided self, with the diametrically opposed forces of her nature and her nurture co-existing in her.

'It wasn't like that,' Jenny said. 'I don't know what you're imagining, but you're way off beam. I could do anything I liked.' Then she smiled and said, 'as long as they didn't know about it.'

'But it must've been awful keeping everything secret?'

'It wasn't that. They didn't know anything about it because life for them never existed outside Balcurran House. Like your Bishop Berkeley, you know, nothing exists if you can't touch it or see it.'

It was startling, this reminder that this crude Jenny had been to one of England's top boarding schools. I asked, 'Why *my* Bishop Berkeley?'

'Oh, people like you always quote Bishop Berkeley. It makes them sound intellectual and they don't have to actually know anything about philosophy.'

That kind of comment must have given the young Jenny's schoolgirl social circle down in the village food for thought. I felt sorry for her, though; it was obvious she'd never really fitted in anywhere. That's what happens when people mess about with other people. It was no wonder she was a bit backward in some ways. She was an odd creature, putting on this rebellious teenager act, and looking about seventeen when she was certainly into her thirties.

Anyway, Jenny took umbrage at what she took to be criticism of the Durrants.

'You must've realized they're innocents,' she said. 'They live through everything that happens and they never even notice. They didn't see it had anything to do with them at all.'

'How could you stand it? I'd have run off.' I was sure I would.

'No you wouldn't,' Jenny said. 'Not with no money, no transport, nowhere to go and no one to go to you wouldn't. Anyway, I couldn't have done that. Still can't. I'm all they've got.'

'Are you serious!' It wasn't even a question, I was so sure she was mocking some conventional middle-class excuse she thought I would have made. I couldn't believe she might mean it.

But Jenny began to look cross that I doubted her. She said, 'They've done everything for me. We're family, aren't we, them and me?' She wasn't fooling. She meant it.

'I know what it's like to have a family,' I said, trying to get back on terms with her. 'It's stultifying. When I was a kid I used to pray my parents would split up, then something exciting might happen.'

'All I know,' Jenny said, 'the Durrants didn't leave me, whatever I did. They could've done but they didn't.'

I tried to put myself in her place and understand her, but I couldn't. I felt she needed rescuing in some way, but she warned me off. She said, 'Don't stick your nose in, right? We all get along just fine as we are. They carry on doing what they think is right, watching over me, and with Charlie I've got a life of my own they don't know about, and what they don't know won't hurt them, right?' Then she asked me not to say anything about seeing Charlie. 'Please, whatever you do, don't mention him to those two,' she said.

I just said, 'It's none of my business what you do,' but I couldn't help adding, 'and none of theirs, either.'

I tried to write down for Alison what had happened, but the scene evaporated when I tried to put it in words on paper. But I kept remembering Jenny's story of the woman locked in the well-house and I felt a cold chill down my spine.

seventeen

Looking back now on what happened, over this distance of years, I can't really recreate the growing certainty I felt during that time at Balcurran House that I was being held prisoner. I knew my fear was irrational. I was not locked up. I was free to wander the grounds, albeit under the cloak of Hilda's suspicion that I was slacking. But I was aware that I could not simply leave. I had no money. I could not telephone for a taxi to take me some place where I could take a bus or train. I would have had to feel much more frightened than I did to write to my parents for help. I couldn't make such an admission of failure in my first independent venture. But at least I did have Alison to confide in. As long as she knew where I was and what happened to me, I could come to no harm.

Was it simply in hindsight that I detect a note of gathering hysteria in my letters to Alison? I know I swung from one irrational extreme to another at the time, but even at my most paranoid, I'm not sure I ever tried to work out in my own mind why the Durrants should want to imprison me. It wasn't the Durrants, plural, I was afraid of, anyway, it was Hilda Durrant, singular. Oh, most singular.

It's hard now to shed the self-possession of years and

empathize with that painfully shy, silly young woman that I then was. A girl who couldn't give credence to her own fears, though at the same time she couldn't dismiss them. It simply seemed impossible that such things could happen to me. Honestly, I didn't have any confidence in my own over-heated speculations, and it would have seemed impossibly rude to demand to go with nothing more than those to go on.

There was also work still to be done on Wadhurst Carpenter. What had happened to break up his close relationship with Cecil Durrant? I had been searching the later diaries for mentions of him without success. He no longer existed for the old man. It was important to me to know. I still saw my book on Wadhurst Carpenter as a way of launching the rest of my independent life. I know I felt guilty that I wasn't being straight with Patience and Hilda. They would have been devastated to know what I was thinking.

Of course I was puzzled that Alison didn't answer my letters. That I couldn't understand. But I knew that the rational explanation was the most likely: perhaps she was more ill or injured than I thought. Or maybe she'd grown out of Gothic tales by this time. Or she simply preferred not to take up the reins of our old friendship. My worst imagining was that Hilda was intercepting my letters and hiding them away to use against me at some later date. I had speculated in one letter to Alison that Cecil Durrant might have been Jenny's father. Hilda would have wanted to kill me for thinking such a thing. If Hilda were reading my letters, I was indeed in danger. But why should she do that? And when it came down to it, what could I do about it? I'd burned my bridges by now, if she'd been reading my letters. And I couldn't just up and go, not with so much still to find out. Also, I trusted Wadhurst Carpenter and he was telling me in his postcards and notes that the Durrants were a kind and loving family, unusual only in their closeness and their mutual happiness. Wadhurst Carpenter knew them from within that circle, as I never could, and he loved them. Who was I, after all, to question his judgement? It was more than my 1966 self could contemplate.

I know that when I woke in the dark early mornings and lay awake waiting for the dawn, I imagined sometimes that Molly and Jenny were in league with Hilda, that they reported to her on what I said and did. I knew these were the melodramatic notions which would melt away as soon as it began to get light, but it's true that my fears seemed very real to me.

Meanwhile one day in that household was exactly like another. One night was exactly like the one before. As soon as the clipped tones of the man on the BBC Home Service finished reading the news, Patience got up and turned off the radio. The Durrants always seemed to feel an almost superstitious urgency about turning off the radio before the next programme was announced.

'Really, I don't know why we listen to the wireless every night,' Patience would say with a sigh, 'such terrible things happen, and there's nothing we can do to help. Those poor Russians, what's going to happen to them with that evil man Kruschev in charge?'

And Hilda would fiddle with that black opal brooch at her throat and say, 'Oh, darling, not evil. You should never say that about anyone.'

'Oh, I forgot,' Patience said, turning her head towards the sound of Hilda's voice, 'Mary Baker Eddy thinks there's no such thing as evil, isn't that so?' Actually, I don't think Hilda was a Christian Scientist but she did tend to come out with uplifting little sayings about willpower and love, and Patience often made sarcastic use of Mary Baker Eddy's name when she wanted to annoy Hilda. I wondered, if I asked Patience straight out if she were blind, if she'd say that Mary Baker Eddy didn't recognize blindness, only moral error.

Patience said, 'Well, Hilda, with all due respect to your guru, as Frances would probably call her, I don't think these people are merely misguided or misunderstood, I think they're evil.' Patience's tone was plainly intended to put a stop to further discussion. I remember being surprised that she knew the word guru. I couldn't imagine I'd used it in front of her. I know I did joke in a letter to Alison that Hilda wouldn't know what it meant. It was a word I used a lot then, but not, surely, to someone like Patience, and her use of it made me uneasy. Of course if I knew then what I know now, I wouldn't have felt uneasy, I would have been stricken with terror.

Hilda was about to launch into a full-scale discussion, or rather a monologue, about using the power of the mind to overcome sin with love, but luckily, hearing her draw breath, the dogs, who had been lying in front of the hearth, jumped up and started to bark, waiting for their walk. It was impossible even for Hilda to ignore the shrill yapping of the Peke alone.

I jumped at the chance to escape. 'I could take them out if you like,' I said.

'Oh, no, that's all right,' Hilda said. She looked startled that I had made the suggestion. Was this evidence that she was holding me some kind of prisoner? Had Patience read that word guru from my letter to Alison? I felt a sharp stab of fear and then dismissed it. Blind Patience could not read.

'I could do with a walk,' I said.

'No,' Hilda said. I almost expected her to stamp her foot, but then she seemed to realize that she was over-reacting. She gripped my shoulder as she walked towards the door and gave it a little shake. It was a friendly gesture, but it was quite painful. I was surprised at the strength in the grip of her fingers, more in keeping with a sculptor than a delicate painter of plants and insects. 'It's dark,' Hilda said, 'and there are some dangerous places if you don't know where you're going. The paths are steep and the leaves have left them slippery. You might fall and sprain your ankle. Or your wrist, and where would your work be then? Or you might get lost.' There was something about the way she said this that made her sound more as though she were casting a spell than giving a friendly warning. I didn't argue.

'We're Englishwomen, we have to secure our castle,' Hilda said with her child-like, sweet, utterly reasonable smile, and I suddenly felt a great desire to say something extremely crude, or swear horribly.

I remember one night as Hilda was about to go out as usual, I asked her, 'Don't you ever cheat, even the least little bit, and cut your rounds short?'

'Oh, no, never. It's like brushing your teeth. It may seem odd to you, but we're set in our ways by now,' she said. 'Father used to walk the dogs and lock up, then when he died I did it for Mother, and we've done it ever since.'

I smiled and said, 'Well I know that if it was pouring with rain or freezing cold, I'd trust to luck sometimes. After all, the gates are locked all day, no one can get near the house unless you go out and let them in, or they've got a key, like

Molly or Jenny, I suppose.' I remember I wanted to stop talking, but my tongue simply ran on like a runaway car down a steep hill.

Hilda interrupted me. I saw that her eyes weren't really blue, they were like thin cloud across the sky, you couldn't see what was going on behind them. But you could see that she saw you when she looked at you; not like Patience, who often seemed not to see what she was looking at. 'Oh, dear, I hope you don't feel shut in here. It would be too terrible if you felt restricted in any way, but you can't be too careful these days. We don't really seem so like jailers to you, do we?' She laughed at the absurdity of such a thought. And I felt disloyal to have written the things I did to Alison.

When Hilda left with the dogs, Patience rose massively from her chair. She moved painfully, her knuckles white as she gripped the arm to pull herself upright. It reminded me that she was an old woman, both the sisters were. Not that Hilda showed any sign of the stiffness or frailty of old age, she moved like a colt.

'Of course, you've only to ask if you want to go out,' Patience said. She was talking to me, but she wasn't looking at me. I moved and she turned her head towards me, but her eyes were blank. Then she straightened herself and once again looked like an old soldier on parade. She went on, 'We're rather short of keys because Jenny lost hers, and you don't have a car, so we never thought ... we thought you'd want to work, so the question never arose. But, my dear, if you feel trapped....' She looked distressed. I knew they thought I'd been rude, but I wasn't sure what I'd done to offend them, unless of course they had been reading my letters!

With that chilling thought in my mind, I was only too glad

to escape upstairs. In my room I didn't put on the light but stood by the window looking out into the garden. A huge full moon hung in the sky above the sea. As I stared down at the dark bulk which was the shrubbery, I saw first the dogs, then Hilda, move into the silver of the frosted lawn like break-away cells on a slide under a microscope. I was uneasy. I can still feel that unease. The moonlight gave a *film noir*-ish quality of corruption to the scene. Whatever I had actually said that evening, I could not rid myself of the feeling that I was now under suspicion in some way. As to who or what might threaten me, I didn't know. I told myself I was being ridiculous, this wasn't a movie chiller, they were two ordinary old ladies shipwrecked in a world they'd lost touch with, simply trying to hang onto what they were used to. They had no hold over me. I couldn't let my overheated fantasies about them drive me away, not when I had still to discover what had happened to estrange their father from his devoted pupil.

In bed, the blankets pulled up round my neck, I watched through the uncurtained window as a black cloud outlined in silver floated across the great vulgar moon. I remembered the shock of looking into Patience's cold clouded eyes and I shivered under the bedclothes. An owl hooted, another answered. Then a vixen called from far away, a sound full of frost and menace. The threatening mystery of the outdoors seemed to have invaded the dark edges of the bedroom. I could not help thinking how cold it must be in the well-house, if poor Carlos was sheltering there, a man from a land full of heat and sun and bright light. The well-house was cursed anyway. Kathleen had come there to throw herself into the black water at the bottom of the slimy, echoing shaft. I felt I understood how Jenny believed she was safe from discovery in the well-house when she went to meet her Charlie there now. The Durrants must have a horror of the place.

eighteen

The next day I wrote a long letter to Alison:

Dear Alison,
Last night I had a horrible dream. Do you think I'm going mad or having some sort of breakdown or something? I know it was only a dream, but it seemed so real. I could see the structure of the pump over the well-shaft silhouetted against the open door of the well-house. It looked like a gibbet. There was a slim young woman leaning out over the shaft. Her fingers were white like bare bones against the stone parapet, and a great bush of red hair hid her face as she looked down into the deep black hole. And then, although I knew I was asleep, I thought, it can't be true, why should Kathleen kill herself? If she'd been suicidal, she'd have done it either before the baby was born, or when she gave her up.

Then I woke up. I was scared stiff of going to sleep again and the dream starting where it left off. I didn't want to see what happened next. I knew where it was taking me. What if ...? No, it couldn't be ... but what if Kathleen had come to make contact with Jenny, to demand her baby back? Wasn't it possible that someone arranged a meeting with her in the well-house and that the same someone pushed her over the parapet and through the rotten wooden cover into the well? I kept telling myself it was only a dream, it wasn't true. At least it wasn't necessarily true. But when I closed my eyes I could see against my eyelids that the huge black shadow looming behind the girl was Hilda Durrant. The blankets were trying to choke me. I was soaked with sweat. I got out of bed. It could be true. After all, why should I be thinking it if it wasn't at least possible?

I stood staring out of the window at the garden in the moonlight, and I told myself: I'm making the whole thing up! I don't want to think that Hilda killed Jenny's mother, it's preposterous. Hilda is a poor lonely old woman who once had psychological problems, a nervous breakdown, that's all. She's a victim. How can I see her as a monster? Is it simply because she was brought up in some freakish fashion? For God's sake, she was brought up in an unusually close and loving family.

There was a huge full moon. I don't know if I dreamed it, or if it was real. It looked like a porcelain plate crazed by the tracery of leafless boughs. It looked menacing like that, spoiled. I still had the childish habit of wishing on the full moon. I went back to bed and wished: Please, let it not be true, let – God only knows what I wanted then, I didn't. Dreaming or awake, I just sort of yearned. I even found myself talking to Wadhurst Carpenter. I was sure I would be safe with him, but I couldn't find him.

In the end it was so cold I knew I was awake. A clock downstairs struck three o'clock. Then I had a thought and I sat up in bed wanting to shout out in relief. Hilda was no murderer. If she had been, she'd have tipped Kathleen down the well and left her. No one would ever have found her. If Hilda had killed her, she wouldn't have been the one to discover her, that proved that she was innocent. Isn't that right?

I was so relieved I could scarcely believe that I could have been so convinced by the silly Gothic horror story I'd been building up in my head. But even so I couldn't leave it, my mind wouldn't let go and returned to it the way you can't stop prodding at a sore tooth with your tongue. I'd let Hilda off the hook unless ... unless she'd been seen with Kathleen, unless there was someone who knew what she had done, so that she had been forced to make up a story to cover herself. But who would have seen her? Patience? Well, possibly Patience, but it wasn't likely Patience would be lurking in the woods. And Jenny was only a little girl. Could she have gone to meet her mother? Jenny? I lay there with my eyes squeezed shut, trying not to hear Jenny's rough voice repeating, echoing through my head, 'Oh, I can do what I like with Hilda, she knows better than to get in my way.'

This morning I'm so tired I can hardly keep my eyes open. I'm sure Freud would have an explanation. Actually Freud would probably have some theory that I'm in love with Wadhurst Carpenter and am subconsciously trying to make him take care of me. I must be feeling better because I'm not taking myself seriously.

Sorry, Alison, I think I'm losing touch with reality. Hilda was particularly nice to me at breakfast, asking if I'm sure I'm not working too hard, I look so tired. Her voice was warm with concern and she gave me a sweet, anxious smile, and there was I staring at her looking for the smallest sign that this gawky old woman fiddling with her black opal brooch, with her glassy blue eyes and wispy grey hair, could be a dangerous psychopath. Oh, no, she wasn't wearing the black opal brooch. She's going to Porterstown this morning and she never wears it when she goes there. That brooch is just something I associate with her now, like Patience's unseeing eyes.

Hilda asked me again how I was getting on with my study of Wadhurst Carpenter, had I found anything new? Of course I was suspicious that there was something behind the question. But I pulled myself together. They don't know I'm reading Cecil Durrant's secret diaries, they think I'm studying his correspondence. I mustn't give anything away, they might be angry knowing that I was reading family secrets – if, indeed, they've ever read the diaries themselves. I suspect they haven't.

I told her I didn't sleep very well last night. I told her that her father certainly mentions Wadhurst Carpenter quite often in passing, in his letters. But of course the comments are out of context, so they don't mean much to me yet. It's going to be a question of fitting the references together to see how important they are. But I did say there seemed to be some sort of break-up between the two men, and Wadhurst Carpenter went missing. I asked her outright if she knew anything about it.

She looked vague and said something about them probably working together and having nothing to say to each other at the time. Then she was all concerned about my not sleeping. She put out a hand as though she was about to feel my forehead for signs of fever, but then withdrew it. She offered to get me something from the chemist, and that was that.

I've run out of time now, but more later. There's something I've got to do and I can't put it off. This is my chance. I can settle this thing once and for all.

nineteen

What did I have in mind? I must have hoped to find something, but God knows exactly what I was looking for. Perhaps I didn't know myself. I can't remember now, but it seemed at the time tremendously significant.

And I do remember what I did.

At mid-morning I heard the revving engine of Hilda's funny little Ford Prefect and a screech of gears as she drove off. I made my way to the courtyard in time to see Jenny close the wooden gates across the archway to the road. Then I watched her go across the cobbles and disappear into one of the ramshackle stables. Good. With her gone, and Patience in her studio, there was no one in the house.

I made as little sound as possible as I went up the stairs and crossed the landing to the door of Hilda's room. The house was unnaturally quiet. When I touched the doorhandle I had to fight an urge to run away. But I had to try to find out for sure, I had to try to put my mind at rest about her. What I expected I don't know. I recall at the time a voice in my ear was telling me that I was being ridiculous even to entertain the kind of imaginings I had spun around a poor old lady. I had a strong sense that I was about to make a complete fool of myself. I told myself that if the door was locked, I'd drop it, I'd forget the whole thing. 'You can't do that,' said the voice in my ear, 'why would the door be locked if she hasn't got anything to hide?'

I wonder why it never occurred to me then that the answer to that question could well be that Hilda didn't trust the peculiar young English visitor who had forced herself on the household with a specious excuse about research and who could easily be a thief.

But it didn't. The door wasn't locked. I opened it and went in.

Hilda's room as I recall was large, light and airy, with a wide casement window. The walls were papered in a pattern of pale yellow roses and there was a magenta motif on the patchwork quilt covering the bed. There were dozens of battered lead soldiers arranged on a dressing table supporting a rococo gilded mirror. I'd expected cool shades of blue and beige and Victorian paintings of a sentimental school, and the girlishness of the room was surprising, it was so child-like and feminine, except for the lead soldiers. The one note of sophistication I saw was the black opal brooch lying in front of the mirror where she'd left it when she went to town in case she tempted the natives to theft.

There were photographs set out on an elegant mahogany chest of drawers, all uniformly framed in polished silver. Many were of one-eyed or torn-eared dogs, but I picked out a sepia version of Cecil Durrant and his bride taken not long after they were married, I guessed: he looking like Methuselah, she like a happy schoolgirl.

There was also a posed photograph of the teenagers Hilda and Patience, in pearl necklaces and perky little hats; another smudged print of them in riding gear standing one on either side of a shaggy pony. And there were several photos of a grumpy child at various early ages who was unmistakably Jenny.

I went to Hilda's writing desk, a Victorian davenport standing close to the window but out of direct sunlight. I lifted the lid of the desk, then flicked through the few papers and used envelopes inside, but there was nothing to help me in my search, they were all recent, or business letters about her work. I wished I knew what I was looking for, but perhaps I would know it when I saw it.

The desk had drawer handles on either side, but only those on the right opened. I started searching them from the bottom. Old pens, a bottle of ink, bills, a bottle of aspirin tablets, nothing of any interest. The top drawer didn't open. There was no keyhole, so it couldn't be locked. I thought it must be stuck, but although I shook and pulled at it, nothing happened. Then I remembered that these desks often had a hidden mechanism inside which opened secret drawers. It wasn't hard to find. I half-opened one of the stationery compartments inside the lid and the drawer was released. I took out the single envelope that lay inside. It was addressed to Mrs Durrant and postmarked Cambridge, Massachusetts, May 1935.

I unfolded two pages of blue paper covered in a looping scrawl written in black ink. The letterhead was printed, Sidney Mynott, Professor Emeritus, Department of Social Anthropology, Harvard University. I started to read. It wasn't easy, the ink had blotched in places, faded in others.

As far as I could tell, Professor Mynott was an old friend and associate of Cecil Durrant's before his marriage. He was presuming on this friendship to write to his widow out of concern, and to offer her any benefit she might take from his experience as a scientist specializing in the study of human behaviour and genetics. His reason for taking this step was news that had reached him through a mutual friend of the late Cecil Durrant and himself that the family intended to adopt and bring up as their own the child of a servant girl and an unknown father. Professor Mynott wrote:

My experimentation and field of study over the many years of my academic career leads me to warn you and your daughters absolutely against such a course of action. It will end in disaster for all concerned, including the child.

Although it is now a fashionable conceit in intellectual circles to maintain that environment breeds consciousness, this is not, in my opinion, supported by any reputable scientific research. Through my own observation I believe that a child is predisposed by its natural parents to develop along the behavioural and social path of its genetic inheritance. Briefly, all efforts to train the child to reflect the interests, attitudes or abilities of your family will be thwarted as the child will revert inevitably to type.

To be blunt, what you propose – to many, undoubtedly, an enlightened and generous gesture – seems to me an act of folly which raises ethical concerns about what, for want of other words, I describe as social engineering. I know that your intentions in this are not cruel or dangerous, but I pray, dear lady, that you will reconsider this project, which may turn out to be both. From a scientific point of view, of course, such an experiment must be exciting, but you and your daughters are not involved in this field of study, and as a scientist myself I believe that it exceeds the bounds of professional ethics. I do not wish to frighten you, nor to thwart a generous and most charitable impulse....

I'd reached the end of the second page. I checked the envelope, then the drawer, but there wasn't any more. My God, I thought, what must Mrs Durrant have felt on reading that letter? What kind of madman was the old Professor, too, with those dreadful Victorian elitist views of his? He sounded like some kind of Nazi. Surely Mrs Durrant's first reaction would be to throw the thing away, to try to forget all about it, but obviously she hadn't, and it seemed that after her death, Hilda had kept it and hidden it away as her secret. Did she read it to herself then and see intimations there of Jenny's development? Did she blame herself for what Jenny had become? To Hilda, what the Professor had written when Jenny was a baby, must have seemed uncanny, only too horribly accurate, if she'd read it for the first time when Mrs Durrant died, which wasn't until after the end of the war, in 1946 or 1947. She'd have known by then what Jenny was like. It seemed to foretell the way she'd become, seeking out the servants to make friends, the ugly way she talked, her rough, aggressive attitudes, the violence implicit in everything she did or said in spite of everything they'd tried to teach her.

I was standing there with the letter in my hand when a gruff voice behind me said, 'So, have you passed judgement and found me guilty of ruining their lives?'

Jenny was standing in the doorway, watching me. I'd no idea how long she'd been there. There was no time to stuff the letter back into the drawer and shut the desk. My heart was pounding and my face was bright red with embarrassment.

Jenny asked, 'What are you doing in Hilda's bedroom?' The girl was enjoying herself. I could tell that she was amused watching me. Her greenish, cat eyes made me feel like a mouse in a trap. I couldn't think of anything to say. I stood there with the opened letter from Professor Mynott in my hands, an obviously private, hand-written letter. Jenny waited.

'I'm sorry,' I said, 'I was—'

'Snooping,' Jenny said.

'Yes,' I said.

'What do you make of the Prof's Awful Warning?' Jenny asked.

Again I didn't know what to say. I was horrified. It was shocking that she should know what was in the letter.

'Oh, don't worry,' Jenny said. 'How do you think I know what's in the letter if I didn't go through their things? If Hilda didn't want anyone to read it, she shouldn't have left it where I could find it. Or you.'

'I'm sorry,' I said again. This time I was offering some vague sympathy to disassociate myself from what the Professor had written.

'Hilda would be shocked to the marrow if she knew you'd been poking around in here,' Jenny said and her voice was no longer gruff. She spoke in something more like standard English, and without any comic intonation. 'She takes it for granted that no one with any manners is the slightest bit curious. The point is, what would Hilda say if she knew I'd caught you here in her bedroom reading her private letters? I mean, everyone has secrets they don't want anyone to know. You'd have to be punished!'

'Punished?'

'Oh, yes.' There was a glint in her eyes. She was enjoying herself.

'Well you'd better not tell her, had you?' I said, keeping my tone deliberately light. 'And I won't tell her about you.'

Jenny looked startled. 'Tell her what about me?'

'About Carlos in the well-house.'

'Charlie? That wouldn't get you very far. She wouldn't believe you.'

'Why shouldn't she?'

'You don't get it, do you? We Durrants don't do that kind of thing.' Jenny laughed at my doubtful face. 'She'd never let herself believe it. We don't tell lies, either, so she'd believe you'd been snooping if I say I caught you. She'd put you down as some sort of degenerate. She'd pity your poor parents.'

But then Jenny lost interest in this game with me. She seemed all of a sudden in a great hurry to get rid of me. 'Come on, clear off,' she said, in her gruff voice, 'I can't hang around blethering to you all day.'

There was nothing else I could do. I put the letter back in the desk and walked out of the room feeling like a naughty schoolgirl caught cheating by the teacher. I wouldn't plead with Jenny not to tell Hilda what I'd done. If she wanted to get me sent away in disgrace, that was up to her.

I spent the afternoon doing research on Cecil Durrant's correspondence with Wadhurst Carpenter. After being caught in Hilda's room, I didn't dare to open the cupboard in the wall of the study to take out the 'secret' diaries, so I concentrated on the box of papers from the drawer of the old man's desk. Thank God he'd meticulously copied his correspondence with Wadhurst Carpenter. Did he preserve his letters to his disciple with the expectation that one day someone like me would be interested enough in the younger man to want to study them. Or did he think that he himself would one day be recognized as the great man. Whatever his reasons, I was grateful that he'd kept those close-scrawled pages, however hard they were to read. And I was rewarded. A letter from Cecil Durrant to Wadhurst Carpenter.

My dear Wadhurst, my dear friend, my eyes are red-raw from reading your manuscript, which I embarked upon two days ago and have been unable to put down except to attend to the necessities of life.

Now I am perplexed as to what to say to you. The Seeds of Knowledge is a book full of wonder, a huge achievement. But I am forced, for your own sake, my young friend, to counsel caution. There are things in this book too frank, too personal, to be placed in the public domain. No good can come of its publication without excising these dangerous passages. Have you given full consideration to the standpoint of the common reader, who comes to your work with no understanding of the nature and reputation of those you write of? I fear, dear friend, that you could lay yourself open to charges of disloyalty to your race and creed. You must surely think again about what you say and what you reveal about yourself in matters of faith and sexual propriety. As it is, I fear to keep it within my house where it might be seen or read by my wife and daughters until such time as you shall have modified the personal revelations therein.

Nearly forty years on, I felt almost nostalgic for the naiveté of the young girl I was when I first read that letter. Cecil Durrant's attitude had seemed to me then like an affront to women in general and the women in his family in particular. The words intellectual fascist and male chauvinist pig had certainly come to mind. We used them very easily then. I can see now that this trivialized our comprehension of the past, But then they tripped off the tongue. I was genuinely puzzled that anyone, not only Cecil Durrant, could have written like that, so oppressively protective of other human beings. And I tried to think of any passage or even suggestion in *The Seeds of Knowledge*, where his reaction might be justified.

I remember my feeling of frustration that I could never understand where they were coming from, men like that. Attitudes had changed so much by the sixties, how could I hope to see what Cecil Durrant had been getting at? Faith and sexual propriety? As far as I could remember, there was no specific mention in the book of either. I thought there'd been episodes when Wadhurst Carpenter, a Christian travelling among Moslem pilgrims, had been obliged to break a journey to observe the strict rules of the *hajj*, but nothing about heathens or savages or anything embarrassingly colonial like that. And I was sure there was no overt sex at all, not even references to the wives of the Arabs who were Wadhurst Carpenter's companions. Some Syrian girls had danced once, on a holiday, but it was a charming scene, quite innocent with no hint of lewdness that I could recall. Wadhurst Carpenter had drawn some conclusions from anecdotal research he carried out into Arab girls' sexual education, but these seemed to me strictly within the bounds of sociological science.

I hadn't understood Cecil Durrant's attitude then, and to be honest, even with all the objectivity of greater age, I don't really understand now. I still can't get inside Cecil Durrant's mind to see what he was afraid of. To me now, though, his attitudes seem like an inevitable part of history, as indeed do those of my own young self. I interpret them as some kind of socio-rational imperative, fuelled by passionate emotion which now seems quite irrelevant to the progress of humanity. At least, though, I do agree with my 1960s self that Cecil Durrant was not like other men, other fathers. But then my understanding was entirely coloured by my own awakened sensuality. I haven't forgotten what that felt like. Sometimes still if I hear an old Righteous Brothers song on the car radio, I have to catch my breath and hold back tears because it takes me back to those times when I expected that love would strike and change me utterly.

Happy days – or so they seem now. At the time I could only work with what I knew. I thought that all I could try to do was understand Patience and Hilda as they presented themselves to me, because what they thought and the way they acted was the best clue I was going to get as to who and what their father was.

twenty

That evening, I felt there was something up. I couldn't put my finger on it, but there was a definite atmosphere. Hilda was behaving in an odd way, on edge and upset. She wasn't wearing her black opal brooch at dinner for one thing, which was unusual. Normally she put it on when she got back from Porterstown. She was distracted at supper that night. Usually she was like a superannuated instructor at one of those schools like Lucie Clayton where there was a right way of doing everything, probably even things like kissing and making love. But this night she seemed to have forgotten the form altogether. She was positively withdrawn.

Anyway it gave me the chance to start my new analytical study, looking at the Durrant sisters as the fruit of their upbringing. Actually there was nothing scientifically esoteric about the way Hilda was upset. The signs were the same as anyone else's. Her eyes were red and her face blotched, in spite of a thick layer of pink powder she'd put on to try to hide that she'd been crying. She said Amen to Patience's grace in a voice thin and wavering with emotion, and then sat poking at the food on her plate, looking down her long nose at it, and not eating anything. Patience sat, impassive like her namesake on the monument. She seemed to be trying to ignore Hilda, so I was the one who asked her if she wasn't feeling well.

I think Hilda was surprised I asked. 'I'm perfectly well,' she said, sounding impatient, but then she seemed to regret her snappy tone. 'I'm not ill, dear, but something very disturbing has happened here, in fact nothing like it has ever happened before in all our years at Balcurran House.'

She looked as though she didn't expect, or want, to be asked further questions, but I was too curious to worry about what she'd consider a breach of good manners. 'What's happened?' I said. 'Is there anything I can do?'

Hilda gave a long, shuddering sigh and shook her head. She was obviously too choked to speak. It was Patience who said, 'Hilda has been robbed.' She made it very clear from her tone that she thought that should be the end of the matter.

But Hilda started to weep again and held a damp handkerchief to her eyes, positively wailing, 'Oh, no, not robbed. Not really robbed, that sounds so much worse than it is. A few of my little treasures have been taken from my room, that's all. Nothing valuable, really, but they were precious to me.'

'Your black opal brooch?'

Hilda nodded, speechless.

'All her jewellery,' Patience said, 'our mother's jewellery.'

I couldn't help being shocked. It was an odd coincidence that Hilda's jewellery should be stolen practically at the same time as I'd had been snooping in her room. I actually thought, God, I'm glad no one except Jenny knew I was there, they might think it was me.

And then the horrible thought struck me that Jenny must be the thief. It had to be her. Why else had she come back to the house? Usually when she was working outside she didn't come in at all. Why else did she go to Hilda's room when she knew the old woman had gone to Porterstown? Jenny had to be the thief, and she knew she'd get away with it because she could tell Hilda how she'd found me searching the bedroom. I didn't doubt she'd say it was me, and Hilda would believe her.

Hilda was still sniffing and trying not to cry. I asked if she'd told the police. That seemed to make her pull herself together. She blew her nose. She shook her head. 'That's not necessary,' she said, 'I've dealt with it already.'

I didn't understand what she meant. I thought she must mean she knew who'd done it.

'There's only one person it could be, dear, isn't there?' She looked up then and I knew she wasn't simply hurt and distressed, she was livid. Really furious. Her mouth was set in a thin line, her eyes narrowed in accusation, and her nose seemed like a pointing, accusing finger. I couldn't meet that awful glare. It seemed to accuse me.

'I didn't take any jewellery,' I said, feeling as if I couldn't get enough air into my lungs.

Both Hilda and Patience looked astonished. 'Of course not, dear, the very idea of it!' Hilda said. She was so startled that she looked like her normal self again.

But I didn't have time to feel relieved, because if she didn't think it was me, then who? Did she suspect Jenny? Anyone who had read Professor Mynott's letter must've expected Jenny to be capable of such a thing.

And then Patience spoke the awful words: 'It's Molly Dunn,' she said. She was silent for a moment. Then she said, 'We are distressed because she has been with us for many years, and we cannot imagine what would possess her to do such a thing, but there is no one else.'

Hilda started sniffing again. 'How could she betray me in this way?'

'Oh no, no, not Molly, I don't believe it,' I said.

Hilda stiffened. 'I hope you don't think anyone in this family would do such a thing? Are you accusing my sister? Or Jenny?'

I hesitated, and I knew that Hilda noticed it and that she'd hold it against me. But I didn't know what to say. I couldn't accuse Jenny without proof. I couldn't even say that Jenny might know something. If I said that I found her in Hilda's room, how was I to explain what I was doing there? Jenny actually had more right to be there than I had.

'What does Molly have to say?' I asked, hoping that she might have some alibi which even the Durrants could not question.

'She has been dismissed,' Hilda said. 'We will have to do without her services.'

'Have you got your jewellery back, then? Did she have it on her?'

'My dear Frances, you surely don't think I searched the woman, do you? She did not give it back. She denied that she had it. In fact she was quite brazen. She laughed and then she looked me in the eye as bold as you please and said "So the apple doesn't fall far from the tree." Then she handed me her apron and walked out. Extraordinary behaviour. What do you make of that?'

There was nothing I could say. I was thinking how terrible for Molly Dunn, how betrayed she must feel. But then I supposed that I, of all people, realized that little Molly Fry-that-was knew the depths of Hilda's capacity for treachery. I made some remark – something about not knowing what Molly could've meant. Hilda looked vague. Patience leaned forward and put her hand with its big broad fingers on her arm.

She said, 'I imagine that she was referring to our late mother, who was a strict disciplinarian with the servants. It is possible that a woman of that type would expect Hilda, who is known to have a soft heart, to be what I think they call a "pushover" when it comes to punishing wrongdoing. So Molly was expressing surprise that Hilda is more like our mother than she had expected. What else could she mean?'

She looked at me, but her eyes were fixed on something behind my left shoulder. It was quite disconcerting to talk to Patience when she spoke in the queer stilted way she did sometimes, like someone quoting from the Bible, and then suddenly firing a straight question she didn't want answered. She'd have done wonders in the Spanish Inquisition. I wanted to ask Hilda, Is that what you think she meant? But Patience sort of threw me off course and when I looked at Hilda she looked blank and began to collect the plates. All discussion was at an end. Poor Molly, it wasn't right she should take the blame. Presumably she was doing it without making more of a fuss for Hilda's sake, to protect Hilda from the truth. Molly must have known it was Jenny, I'd no doubt about that. But there wasn't anything I could do for her.

I thought that perhaps Jenny would own up when she found out what had happened. She could say she borrowed the jewels, thinking Hilda wouldn't mind and meaning to mention it, but it slipped her mind. It wouldn't be difficult for her to make herself seem innocent, and Molly would be reprieved. I decided I had to make Jenny do something and so I waited until the Durrants had carried out their evening ritual of Nine O'Clock News, dog-walking and locking up. I heard them wish each other goodnight and then close their bedroom doors. Then I went downstairs as quietly as I could. I didn't want to have to explain what I was doing.

I made my way through the passage to the back stairs which lead to Jenny's room at the rear of the house, in what must once have been the servants' wing. Jenny liked to be on her own like this, or so Hilda said, because she could make all the noise she wanted and no one could hear. I didn't know what kind of noise Hilda imagined Jenny would make. I doubted if she even possessed a radio and if she did I couldn't see her sitting up at night listening to Radio Luxembourg. But then I didn't know, I didn't know anything about what she was really like.

It was a cold night, and even the inside of the house seemed to be foggy in this part of the building. The flag-stones in the passage were damp and slippery and I'd got my leather-soled slippers on. It was like an ice rink and I was afraid I was going to fall. I knocked on Jenny's door. The sound was feeble and I was afraid she wouldn't hear. But then she opened the door.

'Oh,' she said, 'it's you. What do you want?' She made no attempt to pretend she was pleased to see me. I wondered if she'd thought it might be Carlos. 'You'd better come in,' she said. Her voice was thick as though she had just woken up. She was still dressed in the woolly jumper and baggy cords, though. Maybe she went to bed wearing them because of the cold; I'd been reduced to going to bed without undressing, the house was so freezing.

Inside the room I couldn't believe my eyes. It was crammed with small pieces of furniture and each piece of furniture was covered by knick-knacks, every single inch. There was a settee and an armchair but you couldn't see the colour of their upholstery, only piles of highly decorated cushions, small bolsters, lurid draped chiffon scarves and embroidery. Every other surface, the mantel above the fireplace, the groups of occasional tables and glass-fronted display cabinets, were all smothered with china ornaments, figures of animals and children, Spanish dancers and Red Indian braves, models of scenes from Beatrix Potter and *Alice in Wonderland*. Every wall was covered, not only with small Victorian paintings of little girls and fluffy animals, but with horse brasses and brightly painted plaques showing members of the Royal family. And there was a collection of dolls wearing flamboyant national costumes pinned to the exposed beams on the wall facing the window – a Mexican dancer hung suspended in mid-twirl, a Japanese girl held out a basket of flowers, a scarlet-lipped Greek peasant in a head-scarf carried a bundle of cloth firewood in a pannier on her back. I looked for Scandinavian girls with gold plaits, or the blonde Dutch cheese-maker in her gingham apron, familiar in doll collections, but Jenny plainly had no taste for the fair and bland. All her dolls had flowing dark hair, sly black eyes, and the vivid colouring of gypsies.

The fire had gone out but, in contrast to the rest of the house, this room was hot, absolutely stifling, as though it had been locked up for far too long. There was a constant tinkling in the room, the tiny clash of glass, plastic or metal from assorted mobiles hanging from the ceiling. It was a nightmare.

Jenny asked me to sit down but she didn't sound welcoming. I was afraid to move because my hair had caught in the strings of one of the mobiles and, as I turned my head, I set them ringing and clinking.

'It's like a tinker's caravan,' I said. My God, why did I say that, wasn't her father supposed to have been a tinker? I scarcely dared draw breath for fear of knocking something over and breaking it. I felt gigantic, as though I had lumpy woollen gloves on my fingers and size twelve gumboots on my size six feet.

'So, what do you want?' Jenny asked. 'You didn't defy the rules of the house coming out of your bedroom after locking up time simply for a social visit, did you?'

I was beginning to feel ill, as though the top of my head was emptying. There was a sour taste in my throat, too. I sat down on a pile of cushions that I hoped disguised a chair. My elbow caught the edge of a little brass-topped table and a pack of little china dogs jumped forward. They landed out of place and Jenny came across the room and started to put them back where they belonged. There was no mark of dust to show where they'd been. I was surprised, I'd never put her down as houseproud.

I blurted out why I'd come. I told her Molly had been sacked for stealing some of Hilda's trinkets from her bedroom. I waited for her to say something but she looked politely interested, waiting for me to get to the point. 'We know Molly didn't steal anything,' I said. 'It's not fair.'

'Oh?' Jenny said. 'Do we know that? Did you take them, then?'

'Of course I didn't. But you—'

'You think I stole them? Now, why should you think that? What evidence do you have? I don't know how long you'd been in Hilda's room when I arrived, but I don't accuse you.'

I felt really sick now. I wanted to get up and rush out into the cold night air in the passage but I was afraid that if I moved I'd vomit.

'But I know you didn't take them because nicely brought

up people like you don't do things like that,' Jenny said in her mocking 'English' voice, and then she returned to her gruff brogue. 'I was brought up as good as you, but you suspect me, don't you? And why is that?' Her sharp little chin jutted into my face. 'That's because in spite of all the money the Durrants spent on my education and all the Brownies and the dancing lessons and all the public school twits they tried to pair me off with, even a boring little suburban swot like you thinks I'm common as dirt, isn't that right? You agree with that professor.'

I put up my hands to push her off. 'No,' I said.

'Oh, yes you do. You think I'm a thief because I'm not a lady and had a slut of a housemaid for a mother.' Jenny suddenly broke away and turned her back on me. There was a pause, then she said, 'Don't you?'

At that point I was beginning to get angry. It wasn't worth arguing with her, it was Molly I was worried about. It passed through my mind that I didn't want to argue with Jenny because there was some truth in what she'd said. And I was afraid that that was why I was beginning to lose my temper.

'Do you think Molly did it?' I demanded.

'Since you ask, no.'

'Then you've got to do something. Say something.'

'Then it could only be you or me. And I bet you anything that if you admit why you really think it's me, you'll be far too guilty about being a social snob ever to come out and accuse me. We'd have to say it was Charlie, wouldn't we?'

'Carlos? Do you think it could've been?' For a moment I thought it might be a way to get Molly off the hook. But Jenny jeered at me. 'That would make it easier, wouldn't it? He's a foreigner, isn't he? Except Hilda doesn't know Charlie exists and if she did she'd have the police on him and he'd be thrown out of the country. Not for stealing, she'd probably feel sorry for him about that, because he's down and out, but to put a stop to me having such an unsuitable friend.'

I couldn't help smiling at the way Jenny said 'unsuitable friend', because Hilda's prim and fastidious tones to the life suddenly broke through her familiar growl.

I started to protest, but she was suddenly impatient. 'If you're so bloody bothered about Molly, say it was you. So what if you have to leave the house? You can't really be getting that much help out of those old letters. As far as I can see, you don't even believe in your bloody old book yourself, so why bother?'

I had to go. I had to get out of that stuffy little room with those staring china faces everywhere. But as I went out, I asked Jenny why she'd done it. After all, what did she need with a few old trinkets?

'Sell them, of course,' she said, 'I need the money.' She gave me a sudden gloating grin, an open challenge. 'I'm pregnant,' she said. And then she slammed the door in my face.

twenty-one

The next day, still full of an obscure foreboding, I opened Cecil Durrant's diary for 1921, at the page for 3 August.

A day of trial. Wadhurst Carpenter, whom I love like a son and have long cherished as my friend and pupil, came to me today in great agitation. He revealed that this very night he has an appointment with my Hildina, to meet her on the cliff road, to go away with her and become her husband.

This news has dealt me a great shock. I accuse my once-dear pupil of perfidy that he should thus seduce my child under my very roof. He tells me that such a notion had never entered his mind; that he did not know what Hilda was planning; that he loves her only as part of my family; that though she declared her love for him – it is as a knife in my heart to write these words – he misunderstood both the nature and the intensity of her passion. He had interpreted her preference for him as a schoolgirl emotion, the attachment of a growing child for an older person. He declares himself much to blame, though as he is unmarried I must concede the truth of his claim that he has had no practice with young girls nor knowledge of the female sex to guide him in such a matter. Now Hilda has come to him and revealed her plan, and he, not knowing what else to do, has come to disclose all to me. He is concerned at what might be the effect on Hilda if he tells her that his feelings of love for her are no more than those due to her as a sister, the beloved child of a man he loves as a father.

Then twelve days later, on 15 August 1921, I read:

Dear Mummum braved poor Hilda, who has not left her room these two days, to tell her our decision. She made it clear to the child that though we have reservations about Wadhurst Carpenter's suitability as a husband for a young girl of her age and experience, he being past thirty summers, we are sensible that there was an even more considerable gap in Mummum's age and mine when we embarked upon our own long and fulfilling life's journey together. We feel, in short, that it is only right that Hilda should marry for love and we pray that she and her beloved will be as happy as have been dear Mummum and myself. Wadhurst Carpenter is a good man and we rejoice in their life union. They shall be married, with our blessing.

But dear Mummum has been confounded. Now Hilda refuses to countenance marriage to the man who, as she sees it, has betrayed their love by revealing their secret elopement. Her attitude appears to be that dear Mummum and I have ruined her life. I am much distressed that she can think we do not want her to be happy – which is indeed our dearest wish. She told her mother that no loving parents should contemplate such a marriage for her, that Wadhurst Carpenter is an old man and she much too young to be forced into a loveless union. She hates Wadhurst Carpenter and says, furthermore, that if we loved her we would bar him from our home or any contact with our family.

Then on 16 August 1921:

It is over. My darling Hildina, that blessed child, came to me this morning and promised that it is over. We shed a few tears together. I am sensible indeed of what this, her first passionate emotional attachment, must mean to a loving and natural young woman. I am not too old to remember how it was with my beloved Caroline when she gave up to me the great gift of her heart. I suggested to my Hilda that we should thank God together that He has given her strength in her hour of temptation.

I spent an hour or more this evening alone here in my room wondering at the ways in which our Lord provides His help in our hour of need. I asked Him to keep Hilda in His Heart.

It seemed to come to a head the next day, 17 August 1921:

Duty to family mirrors duty to God, and I have no choice. Hilda is my child, she is adamant. Wadhurst Carpenter, whose affection and knowledge have sustained me in friendship over long years, will never come here again. He has undertaken to have no further contact with my family in any way at all. I pray that Hilda may understand one day how much it has cost him and me for her sake. I told my friend that I must sacrifice our great love and friendship to Hilda's continued happiness and respect for me and dear Mummum, and he did not dispute my decision. We wept.

twenty-two

Seated on the bed in my parents' room that had been their marital kingdom for so many years, with the fragments of my own youthful hopes strewn over the coverlet, I felt a pang of nostalgic pain at the memory of those entries in Cecil Durrant's old diary. It takes me by surprise. I hadn't realized how long it is since I felt the first thrill of academic discovery. I remember it now like the stab of a knife, the excitement of that first uncharted scholastic revelation I'd ever made.

This was why Wadhurst Carpenter had disappeared from Balcurran House.

Looking back I can say now that it was the moment when I knew that I had found my vocation. Funny really, it was the instrument that finally liberated me from the familial dependence which this now inscrutable bedroom meant to me then. I knew certainly that the pursuit of this excitement was what I wanted to do with the rest of my life and no one could stop me.

I felt retrospective sadness for Hilda. I think at the time I found her passion rather absurd, too grotesque for pity. And of course I didn't want to hear about unreciprocated love, consumed as I was by dreams of a sweet, passionate love affair of my own as soon as my independent life got under way. A love affair with a man who, in my own mind, I thought would be a lot like Wadhurst Carpenter.

Poor Hilda, how she must have felt betrayed. Of course she said she hated Wadhurst Carpenter, what else could she do? She'd loved him enough to plan to elope with him, she'd wanted to spend the rest of her life with him, sharing the adventures that were left to him, and then warmed by his memories as he raced before her into an old age when she would show her devotion by caring for him. She must have loved and wanted him desperately because she had clearly made all the running. What an idiot she must have felt when he went to her father. And how exciting it must have been for a girl like that, a girl of only seventeen, thinking she was seducing the great adventurer, running away to be together, risking all for love. Except he wouldn't do it.

There had been something else at the time, though. I'm trying to remember. Something in the diary? No. Something about the way I'd discovered the new material about Wadhurst Carpenter? I know that when I sobered up a bit from that first intoxicating moment of discovery, I thought it had all been a bit pat. Contrived. Yes, that was it. Someone else had been using Cecil Durrant's desk, I was sure of it. The night before I'd cleared away the papers I was working on, as I always did. I'd locked the 'secret' diaries back into the wall cupboard and hidden the key in its drawer before I went to get ready for the seven o'clock gong as I did every night. But that morning the 1921 diary was lying on the desk open at the entries concerning the seventeen year old's love affair with Wadhurst Carpenter. The wall cupboard was locked. The key was in its usual place in the desk drawer. Had I actually forgotten to clear the desk when I finished work? If not, someone who knew about the diaries had deliberately left this one for me to find. But who? As far as I knew, no one else went into the study.

I searched the room, feeling rather absurd, looking behind the curtains and under and behind the furniture. I don't know what I would have done if I'd found someone hiding there, but it made me feel better once I was sure the study was empty. I felt even more absurd after I'd spent a good fifteen minutes more thinking about what had happened. This wasn't my room, it wasn't my house, there was no reason at all that Patience or Hilda or even Jenny, Durrants all, shouldn't read one of Cecil Durrant's diaries and leave it open on the desk. It was something so natural that I knew I couldn't even question them about it. But if that entry was intended for me, what was someone trying to tell me? And why? Even more intriguing, who was it? Not Patience, I thought, for I was sure she could not see to read her father's writing. Not Hilda, she would hate my knowing her secret. Unless she hankered for some kind of recognition of her connection with a great man. That did seem possible to the young and inexperienced young woman I was then.

twenty-three

A day or two later, I wrote another long letter to Alison, but about something else that had happened.

Dear Alison,
I'm writing this in my room in the early hours because I've got to get something off my chest before anything happens to stop me telling you.
I went into the little drawing room at lunchtime. Patience was there already. We were waiting for the gong for lunch, which was late. Since Molly Dunn left, meal-times aren't always quite so rigid as they used to be. Patience did not look at me as I came in. She was holding a trap where a mouse was caught by one leg. It struggled and squealed. Patience grasped the little creature carefully as she pulled back the spring to release it. Then she smashed its skull with a chop of her hand. I heard the bone crack. The pathetic slightness of the sound added to the horror. I made some sort of noise. I thought I was going to be sick.
Patience turned to me. She smiled at me. 'Oh, there you are, Frances,' she said. I mumbled something. 'What's the matter?' she asked. Then she shrugged, ignoring the

mouse's body. 'Oh, that?' she said. 'What did you expect? Its leg was caught. Mice are pests.'

'But maybe it would've recovered,' I said.

'Recovered?' she said. 'It was maimed. It had to be destroyed. Once something is maimed like that, it's life wouldn't be worth living.' Then she gave a long, resigned sigh. 'You're shocked,' she said. 'But this is the kinder way.'

I blurted out, 'But it was the way you did it. It was like an execution.'

'You're young,' she said, 'you're sentimental. You don't think it's right that an old woman like me should be able to crack a mouse's skull, isn't that so? Oh, yes, I know you think I'm too old to be able to do much, it's no good denying it.'

She paused, as though to give me the opportunity to deny it, then went on in a quiet, flat, tone, 'It comes to all of us, my dear. I was young once. You find that hard to believe, don't you? But I was, and I haven't forgotten.'

Alison, I can't get the scene, and the flat way she said what she said, out of my mind. It was a bit too Gothic even for you. Anyway, there's something else I have to get off my chest.

The last few days, I've been feeling that maybe I'm coming down with flu. It's as though all my joints need oil, my brain feels waterlogged, and I don't feel like doing anything much. That's what I thought until yesterday – that I'd caught some sort of a bug – but suddenly at supper last night my head started throbbing and I had these vicious cramps in my stomach. The sight of the food on my plate made me feel so nauseated that I had to leave the table. When I came back, Hilda looked down that long nose of hers at me as though I was a specimen and said, 'I hope it isn't something you ate, dear?'

And then Patience put down her knife and fork and folded her napkin and gave a funny little smile and said, 'Hilda's worried about her cooking now Molly's gone. She doesn't think of herself as a good cook and she's afraid she may have put something she shouldn't in the stew. It wouldn't do if you thought she was trying to poison you, would it?'

Hilda gave Patience a look and then with her sweet little smile she said, 'Are you sure you're not using poor Frances here to test one of your plant extracts for toxic effects, dear? That seems to me a far more likely cause than my cooking.'

As soon as I could I went to bed and it was so cold and I was shivering so much I just got under the bedclothes with all my clothes on. And then there was a knock at the door and Hilda came in with a mug of hot milk, which I hate. The sight of it nearly made me throw up again. I couldn't let her see I hadn't undressed so I kept the blankets pulled up to my chin instead of taking the mug, and in the end she left it on the bedside table. I thought she'd never go, and, between you and me, after she'd gone, I got up and tried to lock the door so she couldn't come back and check I'd drunk the hot milk, but the lock doesn't work, so I tipped the filthy stuff down the basin and ran the tap to flush it away. When I started to rinse the mug, I saw this grainy residue at the bottom. Now I can't help wondering – it sounds so crazy I can hardly write this – but I can't help thinking maybe Hilda's poisoning me.

It all fits, you see. I started feeling ill just about the time Molly went and Hilda started doing the cooking. I think *she's been putting the weedkiller or rat poison into my food so that I get a cumulative dose. Otherwise it would be hard to explain the sudden death of a healthy young woman like me without an autopsy, but if she does it little by little I could be ailing for weeks and then an unsuspecting local doctor wouldn't think much of it.*

I can imagine you're thinking I'm going off my head, and I know my symptoms could be flu. But what about that sandy powder at the bottom of the mug? Alison, why would anyone want to kill me? Do you think Hilda has discovered I've read Cecil Durrant's diaries and thinks I've found out some shameful secret? Is there still some shameful secret I've missed so far? But surely that's not enough to make someone want to kill me. I must get out of this place.

P.S. late morning: Just to tell you I woke up feeling much better. I wasn't very hungry but I went down to breakfast and Hilda positively glowed with pride at my recovery. She kept going on about there being nothing like hot milk and aspirin to sweat out an infection. I suppose it could've been aspirin, or is she covering her tracks and I feel so much better because I didn't ingest any of her beastly arsenic? I'm so confused, I can't think straight. What do you think?

twenty-four

It's easy enough now, so many years on, to tell myself that I didn't believe Jenny when she said she was pregnant. I did think that she showed little sign of being out of her mind with worry and fear at the thought of Patience and Hilda finding out, but that was all. Whenever I saw her, she had a silly happy smile on her face making her look quite daft, and that seemed logical enough to my sketchy knowledge then of the joys of coming motherhood. As a matter of fact, it still does, I suppose, to judge by the young women I see now in a similar state.

On the other hand, I didn't see Jenny as one to show her feelings to a stranger. On the whole I decided that she had probably said that she was going to have a baby to get my attention. The way I saw it then, she'd never mixed with women her own age, she probably didn't know what else to say just to start a conversation. She'd think sex and childbirth were sure-fire subjects for girl-talk. How could she know that I had no interest in the subject at all? At that stage of my life I repudiated parenthood. I did not find children appealing at all. People were always telling me I'd change my mind once I found the right man, but on the contrary, that is the one issue on which I never altered. But I was well aware that most women thought having a baby made them interesting.

Jenny and Carlos were having sex, it would be surprising if an innocent like her didn't get pregnant. You couldn't get condoms or any other form of birth control in Ireland then.

I remember thinking that I should try to talk to Jenny about it. But I kept putting it off. Everything seemed too much effort. I wasn't getting very far with my own work in spite of spending more hours than ever poring over Cecil Durrant's diaries. There was something wrong with my memory. I'd read for an hour and then realize that I'd spent most of the day before studying the same passages. These symptoms I thought must be the after-effects of not being well.

But then one day I found myself with Jenny in the kitchen peeling vegetables for Hilda to cook for supper. Jenny had volunteered, to Hilda's obvious amazement, and when she demanded that I should help her, I took it as a sign that she wanted to talk to me. I felt I couldn't refuse, though it wasn't a good moment. I was tired and would have preferred to tackle her away from the house.

Jenny took her time getting to the point. First we had to go through with the ritual grumbling about why shouldn't I help, why should she do all the dirty work, who said she'd got to be the servant? Then she blurted out, 'It's not my fault Hilda sacked Molly. I didn't think she'd go that far. It'll blow over. Hilda will forgive her.'

I didn't say anything. I kept my head bent, scraping mud off the potatoes.

At last Jenny asked, 'What would you do?'

'If I were you? I'd tell Hilda you did it. Then she could ask Molly to come back. You know Hilda would forgive you long before she'll forgive Molly.'

'I don't mean that,' Jenny said. 'I mean about me. About being the way I am.'

I looked at her. She was concentrating very hard on taking an eye out of a half-peeled potato. I remember thinking she must be going to meet Carlos later, she'd taken some trouble with her appearance. She'd washed all that red hair, and she'd powdered her nose and chin, which usually looked shiny as though she spent too long in the cold. But the lime-green sweater she was wearing looked pathetically home-knitted. I wondered if Hilda had made it for her. I had to say something, the silence was becoming painful. In the mood I was in, my first reaction was to admit that in Jenny's place, all I would have been able to think to do would be to run away or kill myself, but it seemed better not to say so to her.

'You've got to help me,' she said, 'you're the only person who can.'

For the first time I was convinced that she really was pregnant. She was terrified, however well she hid it. I didn't know how to comfort her. I couldn't hug her. I'd feel awkward touching her. And Jenny was the sort of person who could easily hate being touched.

'Of course I'll help you, if I can,' I said, 'but what can I do?' I looked at Jenny's face and saw what she was thinking. 'Oh, no,' I said, 'not that, you can't expect me to do that. I can't tell them for you.'

'Don't you see,' she said, 'it would be easier coming from you. You could say you'd noticed something, was it possible someone had ... well, had taken advantage of me? They think I'm a bit backward, you know, they think that's why I never got on with the people at school and why I always liked being with the servants better than with them. And if they thought I'd been raped, they couldn't be so angry with me, could they?'

It comes back to me vividly how horrified I'd been, and she said it so casually. 'But Jenny, you can't do that,' I said. 'They'd get the police and they'd probably accuse someone. They could even accuse Carlos.'

'Well, then, I'll have to tell him to go away before the Gardí start looking.' Her voice didn't falter. I wondered if she had any real feelings for her lover at all.

'Jenny, what do you really want to happen? Do you want the baby? I mean, if you could marry the father, would you want it?'

'I want Charlie,' Jenny said. 'I love Charlie and I want him, I don't care about anything else. It's a way of getting him, isn't it? We can get married and have a little house some-where and I could do Bed and Breakfast and Carlos would get a job and go out to work each morning like anyone else....' She drew breath for a renewed bout of tears.

'They wouldn't let you marry him, however pregnant you are, if you say you were raped,' I said. The look on her face made me relent. 'What does Carlos have to say about the baby?' I asked quickly.

Jenny started to fiddle with a loose thread in her cardigan. She said nothing.

'You haven't told him, have you?' I said.

'Didn't you read the diary? I left it out for you to read. About that man Hilda wanted to marry? The one who ran away when she was willing to elope with him? Don't you see, that's like me and Charlie? I'm afraid he'll leave me.'

So that was all there'd been to the diary mystery, it was Jenny's clumsy attempt at communication. I wondered then if she had read all the diaries. She was a natural snoop. 'You've got to tell Carlos,' I said.

'No. Not yet. It's difficult. His English isn't very good.'

'He's got a right to know if he's going to be a father.'

'Oh, God, don't you know anyone? You know what I mean? You're English, you must know what to do.'

'For goodness sake, Jenny, don't even think about it, you could die. It's against the law, you could go to prison. And anyway, of course I don't know anyone. What gave you the idea I might?'

'I've got the money. That's why I stole Hilda's jewels. And I've been saving up. I thought you'd be sure to know someone and we could pretend I was coming to stay with you in England.'

I could imagine what my parents would make of a pregnant Jenny coming to stay, but it was no laughing matter. 'Jenny, stop it. It's out of the question. You'll have to tell Carlos, see what he's got to say.'

Jenny tipped potato peelings into a bucket and slammed it down beside the sink. She looked more sullen than ever. I couldn't help thinking that if I were Carlos, I'd only have to see that look on her face and I'd disappear back to Spain as fast as I could.

'I tell you, I've tried to tell him,' Jenny said.

'Well, we'll have to get a Spanish dictionary and look up the words,' I said.

'It's not that.' Jenny shrugged. Her ruddy complexion was gone. She was pale. 'He understood. He didn't believe me.'

'What do you mean? Why shouldn't he?'

There was something about Jenny's voice, though, which made me stop. She tried to look defiant, but her face crumbled and she was weeping again.

'It's all right,' I said. 'You can tell me. Why didn't he believe you?' Jenny gulped and gasped, but said nothing.

I rummaged in my pocket and found a Kleenex. She wiped

her eyes, even managed a wan smile. 'You sound like Hilda,' she said, and then could not stop herself, the tears poured from her eyes again.

To be honest, I wanted to shake her. I felt sorry for her, of course, but she irritated me with all her drama and self-absorption. I told myself that she'd talk when she was ready. And in the end, it came out. The time I'd seen them in the well-house had been the first time they went all the way. They'd been meeting for months, but that was the first time. I'd wanted to laugh, I'm afraid. She'd really had me fooled. But it wasn't funny when I looked at her stricken face. She wasn't the only girl who thought you had a baby every time you made love. Who would have told her the facts of life? Certainly not Patience and Hilda, they'd have been too embarrassed, even if they knew. Perhaps they thought knowing such things was part of her genetic inheritance.

Anyway, Jenny had been defiant. 'I've read books,' she said. I suppose that in the kind of novels she read girls always did get pregnant the first time. She said, 'Charlie got angry. He said it couldn't possibly be his. He said he wasn't falling for that trick. I haven't seen him since, and I want him back. I know now I'm not really pregnant, but I thought if you told Hilda I was, she'd believe you and make him marry me, to save the Durrants' face. Hilda knows what it's like to be in love, she'd have to make him marry me.'

I told her what I thought she wanted to hear, that Carlos would be back. He'd realize she hadn't been with anyone else. How could she? She was practically a prisoner at Balcurran House and he knew it. In the end I convinced her.

She rushed off to the well-house, presumably to wait for him. Hilda came back then and thought Jenny had left me with all the work. I was afraid she would start searching for her and find out about the trysts at the well-house. So I lied for Jenny, saying we'd finished and she'd gone to work in the garden.

Hilda said, 'She'd always rather be up to her elbows in mud outside than working in the house, the dear child. You'd never think she did a *cordon bleu* course when she left school.' She began to busy herself collecting the pans she would need to cook supper. 'She never offers to do the cooking. She seems actually to be happier doing the rough work. I fear for her complexion.'

'Perhaps she thinks that's how she can be most helpful to you,' I said, and I didn't try to hide a hint of reproach in my voice. In Hilda's eyes, poor Jenny couldn't seem to do anything right. 'She's so fit and strong, you don't need a man about the place when you've got her here,' I added.

'As long as she's happy,' Hilda said. She went to the stove. I was sure that, as she turned away, I heard her say under her breath, 'What's bred in the bone.' She sounded puzzled, sad.

twenty-five

I went on writing to Alison because I needed to get the things I told her off my chest, but it was getting beyond a joke that she never answered my letters. I'd obviously failed to make her realize how important it was for me to be able to try to explain everything to her and know she understood. She probably thought I was crazy to be so suspicious, and after another Balcurran House evening, I began to think I was.

All evenings dragged at Balcurran House, but this had been worse than anything I remembered. I sat with Patience and Hilda in the small drawing room, holding an empty coffee cup and waiting for the chimes of Big Ben and the Nine O'Clock News to bring relief. Hilda was working at a piece of needlework, peering down over her long nose at a complicated fold of material she was sewing. Her thread kept breaking and each time, with a small intake of breath, she dropped the folds, carefully re-threaded the needle, then picked up the cloth again and anchored it in her big blunt fingers. I must say I admired her persistence; I'd have started to swear, or contrived to rip the material apart and spoil it.

Worse still, each time Patience heard the intake of Hilda's

breath, she said, 'Oh dear, poor Hilda, not another broken thread,' then returned to the old copy of the *Irish Field* that she was reading, or pretending to read, because she wasn't turning the pages.

I was so preoccupied thinking my own thoughts that I almost missed the strokes of Big Ben. I heard the news and instantly forgot everything the newsreader said. I jumped when Hilda, with a great slithering of material, got up to turn off the radio. 'Time to take the doggies out,' she said, 'poor little things, they've been so good waiting all this time.' She said the same thing every night. The dogs jumped up and yapped as they always did.

'And I must get ready to lock up,' Patience said, rising painfully to her feet and steadying herself on the arm of her chair. As usual.

'You look as though you're ready for bed, Frances,' Hilda said. 'I believe you were actually nodding off during the news. You get off to your room. A good night's rest will do you good. Come along, doggies.'

The dogs ran barking to the door, throwing themselves at it in their eagerness to get out. I heard the back door slam and then a crescendo of barks as the animals raced across the lawn towards the wood. A sorry lot of canine cripples they may have been, but there was nothing wrong with the barking equipment of any of them – unfortunately.

By the time they were out of earshot, Patience had disappeared too. It sounds fanciful, but the house suddenly seemed to be holding its breath, the silence was so unnatural. Then a gust of wind blew rain against the window, and a tossing branch scratched the glass with a sound that put my teeth on edge. I fled to my room and shut the door.

Even in bed, I couldn't concentrate on my book. It was a

D.H.Lawrence – *Women in Love* – and it was hard to read it without getting diverted into thinking about sex. Cecil Durrant would have had a fit at the very thought of Mr Lawrence. Funny to think they inhabited the same world at the same time.

The other thing that was making it hard for me to concentrate tonight was thinking about Jenny. She went off to the well-house before supper to wait in case Carlos came to make it up with her. I knew she wanted to be alone, but that place must be spooky at night. She'd think every creak and rustle was Carlos arriving, and she'd be devastated each time when it turned out to be the wind or some animal foraging. It was a blustery night with bursts of heavy rain, and it was bad enough sitting in the bedroom with the wind whining in the chimney. I could hear the sea pounding the rocks like distant gunfire. Frankly, if I were Carlos, I'd have left my reconciliations with Jenny until the weather improved. Poor Jenny, I could imagine how she felt, sitting there alone with the whole of the rest of her life seeming to rest on seeing Carlos again.

I put down my book to throw a shoe at the wall. There were mice behind the wainscot. I'd never heard them making so much noise as they did that night, but I suppose I was usually asleep. It was two o'clock in the morning. I'd be useless in the morning if I didn't get some sleep. Jenny probably gave up on Carlos hours ago. She was probably asleep in bed by now.

I was just about to put out the light when I heard noises outside the window. I couldn't pretend it might be the mice so I went to look out and got a fusillade of gravel hurled towards me. And then moments later Jenny appeared over the sill. She'd climbed up the wisteria. She somersaulted over the windowsill into my room as though she'd every right to be there, and then she said, 'God, it's cold in here,' and she pulled the coverlet off my bed and wrapped it round herself.

My face hurt from the gravel. 'I don't know why you don't come through the door like anyone else,' I said. 'I know you've got your own key to the house.'

'They lock your bedroom at night. Didn't you know?'

No, I didn't know and I knew the lock was broken so it wasn't true. Jenny seemed to lie for the sake of it sometimes.

She sat on the edge of the bed and, I must say, she looked positively radiant. It was a bit galling at that time of night, even the shadows under her eyes looked artistic. She had that tremendously flashy hair and there was this sort of glow about her. I'd never seen Jenny look happy before, and I suppose she was happy. It gave me quite a pang, actually. I envied her and I felt sorry for her at the same time.

She sat there and just sort of grinned at me with a silly smile until in the end I had to say something. I asked if Carlos had come, though of course I knew he must have done. And she hugged herself in my bedspread and looked like someone about to start singing about wonderful, wonderful everything in a musical and she said, 'Charlie loves me. We're going to be married.'

I must have looked as dumbstruck as I felt. I was horrified, but she said, 'I know what you're thinking. You think they won't let me marry him?' I told her not to rush into anything, wasn't it enough for them to be together?

And she said, 'No, it isn't enough.' Then she seemed to decide that she had to explain. 'All I want is what other people take for granted,' she said, 'marrying the man I love and being a family. They can't stop me. I'm thirty-one.'

I kept trying to tell her the Durrants wouldn't allow it, that she depended on them for everything. If she told them about Carlos, they would stop her seeing him, but when I said so she kept repeating they couldn't do that and she and Charlie would run away together and get married in secret, and what could the Durrants do, anyway? And I heard myself saying, 'I'm afraid they'll get rid of him.' And suddenly it felt as though the walls of the room were closing in, and it was terrifically cold and there was a really eerie feeling of menace.

Except Jenny didn't seem to notice, she just went on about how Charlie would always stick by her, the Durrants couldn't do anything. She wasn't even taking it seriously, she made a joke, 'You don't think they'd murder him, do you?'

She didn't like it that I didn't laugh when she said this, I could tell, but then I said something about how he hadn't got the right papers, they could get him sent back to Spain. Or they could take her away, abroad. She gave me a funny look when I said that, like a cat's stare, and said, 'You don't like them, do you?'

I protested that of course I liked them, they'd been terrifically kind to me. She kept insisting that though they'd be a bit shocked, at least Hilda would understand. But if, because she'd read Cecil Durrant's diary for 1921, she thought that Hilda would be on her side because as a young girl she'd wanted to run away with Wadhurst Carpenter, she was making a serious mistake. That had been a disaster and, I was sure, had soured romance for Hilda. Hilda's lover had betrayed her and that could make her want to protect Jenny against Carlos. I said so to Jenny and she started to argue about it, but then suddenly she stopped whatever she was going to say, and she looked a bit uneasy and changed tack. She said, 'That explains something. Once when I was a kid, a strange man came to the house. It was in the afternoon, and Patience was working. He came to the kitchen door, which was queer for a visitor, and Molly said Mrs Durrant wouldn't see him and he must go, he knew he shouldn't be there. And he said he'd come to see Hilda and he was quite upset. He seemed like an old man to me, and I thought it was funny because he was very upset and I'd never seen a grown man upset like that before.'

I asked Jenny if he'd gone away.

'No,' she said, 'not then he didn't. Molly took him to hide in the well-house and it was odd because the man seemed to think that was quite normal, which of course it wasn't. Molly didn't know I followed them there and then she saw me and she told me I must never tell anyone that the man came to the house, he used to be a friend of the family but there'd been a rift and he'd gone away. And then we went back to the kitchen and Hilda was there and Molly told her about the man and said he was waiting to see her and Hilda went all stiff and said Durrants didn't go behind people's backs to meet men like that, and she said Molly deserved to be dismissed for what she did except she didn't want to upset Mrs Durrant with the knowledge that *that man* had been there. I couldn't think what he'd done that was so awful no one would ever forgive him. That must've been *the man*.'

I saw what she was getting at, but it seemed a long shot. 'If it was Wadhurst Carpenter, you must have been very young. Are you sure it was him?'

'I told you I was young. But I do remember, I'm not making it up.' Her voice was rising and I told her to calm down, and I suppose actually it was all right to say it was a long shot, but who else would it have been?

Jenny turned sulky. 'Don't believe me if you don't want to,' she said. 'But that wasn't the only time, either. Molly Dunn told me he'd been before. They turned him away then, too.'

'What do you mean?'

She had a mulish expression on her face. If I wanted to hear what she had to say, she was clearly inclined not to tell me. Then she grinned, and said, 'Molly told me he'd come to the funeral. Cecil Durrant's funeral. But Mrs Durrant had him thrown out of the church. That's what Molly said, anyway.'

She wouldn't say any more. I returned to the subject of Carlos and Hilda. She agreed Hilda wouldn't come round to her marriage, then she said, 'But I know what happened to her, how the family ruined her life, and I'm not going to let them do that to me. I'm marrying Charlie whatever anyone says.'

Here, I thought, was this poor girl who was practically a recluse in this place and she'd found a man she loved and even if it didn't have much chance of working out, surely she was entitled to what happiness she could get. She wasn't likely to get another chance. But why couldn't I encourage her without this foreboding I had that if she went ahead something awful would happen? I still remember the feeling of menace I had talking to her in my bedroom. Or was it the effects of too little sleep and those bloody mice scaring me half to death?

Jenny left and I knew I wouldn't sleep. I felt very uncomfortable about my position in the house. I was beginning to feel like a voyeur and I seemed to have got a long way from my real interest in Wadhurst Carpenter. It even occurred to me that there was something almost perverted about my curiosity about the Durrants. I hoped that wasn't why I was interested in Jenny.

twenty-six

Among the pile of letters Hilda had given me to study, I found a letter from Caroline Durrant. It was dated 13 March 1924:

Beloved,

I am writing to you on the eve of the thirtieth anniversary of our marriage, that day when my happiness was born. Tomorrow there will be celebrations amongst us all, and rightly so, for Patience and Hilda are the blessed flowering of our union. Yet this is also our day, yours and mine. Every year on this day I think back over our long happy times together to that Italian summer hillside shimmering in the heat of the afternoon sun. I recall my first sight of you, so thin and tall with your red beard, when I spied you coming down the track from the Villa Previ high on the steep slope above the sea to visit my father. And I remember how the sight of you took my breath away, and how it seemed to me that I knew in that moment, that you, my darling one, would be the whole of my destiny. Without your presence, since that day, my life is empty and meaningless, and when thus alone, I await your return as one adrift, until you come back to me to hoist the sails

*of our family vessel and set our course home. You know,
of course, that I love you as the other half of my whole
being, so that since the day we met there has been no need
in my life for anyone or anything beyond you and our children, for I live in my love for you, and your love for me
gives me life itself.*

I'd forgotten, but re-reading that letter now, after all these
years I remembered how embarrassed I'd felt as I first read
it. It was too personal, and the sentiment, or at least the
words she used to express the sentiment, were so out of date
that they seemed absurd to me. More than that, inexperienced as I was then, I was definitely hostile to something in
that letter I still can't altogether put my finger on, something
oppressive about her love for her husband. It occurred to me
that perhaps she resented her daughters as a dilution of her
relationship with Cecil Durrant. I suspected the letter was
manipulative, not written from a joyful heart.

After reading it, I tried to forget all about it, I do remember
that. What she wrote had nothing to do with Wadhurst
Carpenter, or even the aspects of Cecil Durrant's life which
interested me. I was kidding myself, I can see that now,
nearly forty years after I first read it, because I'd been fasci-
nated by the unlikely romance between the crusty
middle-aged recluse who'd come down the mountain to visit
General Willoughby-Ingram and with a few words captured
the heart of his youngest daughter. The chapter of the book
I'd started to write, the badly-typed foreword on the
yellowing foolscap pages about Cecil Durrant's meeting with
Caroline Willoughby-Ingram, aged 20, proved where my real
interest lay. I have no idea now how I planned to connect it
to the story of Wadhurst Carpenter's life. I hadn't been able

to decide if it was the most romantic love affair I'd ever heard of, or an obscene abuse of male power. It had seemed at the time a mighty metaphor for the dilemma of 1960s women. Funny, I can't even see it now. As for the Caroline Durrant letter, I suspect that most normal people would have felt warmed by the loving simplicity of the message, so why did it make me feel apprehensive, almost fearful? And then I realized, it's the sort of letter my mother might have written to my father, that's how she felt about him. And even now, with both my parents dead, I feel threatened by it, excluded.

In 1966, I did wonder how Hilda and Patience would react to their mother's letter. As usual, when I started thinking about the Durrants at that time, I tried to analyze their feelings by speculating on my own. Or was it the other way round – did I analyze what I was feeling by speculating on them? I know that letter confirmed for me that I was justified in believing that the bonds of family were invariably too constricting to allow a child to be herself; I thought of the child as female then because I believed this specially true of girls. I had no conception, of course, how small my experience was then. I did as my mother's adage instructed, 'Speak as you find.' Another of her favourites, 'Judge that you be not judged', might have fitted the case just as well, but understanding that was beyond me in those days. Anyway, the Durrant parents took it for granted that their love defined their children and would make them happy. But it stopped them living. It created barriers against everyone outside, nipping in the bud all experience, all experiment and excitement. There was no need for anyone or anything else within a family united by that love. And it made a monster of the ungrateful family member who deliberately wanted to break it to pieces, wantonly, simply to see what would happen next. So it demonized the rebellious child: Hilda Durrant and Jenny – and me!

But reading that letter again, I began to wonder about Caroline Durrant's life, about the carefree Victorian miss who fell in love with a red-bearded eccentric she saw striding down a mountain track, as she leaned dreamily on a stone balustrade in the hot sunshine of an Italian afternoon. Had that young girl always contained the middle-aged woman who wrote that love letter to her ageing husband in immaculate copperplate script in black-opal ink now sparkling iridescent against the yellowing page? I couldn't accept it. That adolescent Caroline I imagined was not born to be Mrs Durrant; she was made into her. Did she change willingly? Anything else was too sad to contemplate. She would have been quite different married to another man. And then I remembered from my own script, how she'd protested about Cecil Durrant's servants stealing his food – 'that's terrible, you can't let them get away with that.' That's the Caroline to whom Cecil Durrant would never dare reveal that he had lost the faith that had been the structure round which they had both built their life.

I tried to banish my niggling doubts. I still preferred my unformed, carefree adolescent to the bourgeois moralist. I'm afraid, though, that it's a failure of logic to accept that something is so because I passionately wish it to be. That's still a tendency I have to watch in my work, and I had it then.

True, now I think back, when I first read the letter, my mind had been full of another missive, one written out of a different kind of love.

Jenny had come in as I finished reading Caroline's letter. I tried to hide it, but she didn't even notice. She was flushed. 'I've got to see you,' she said. 'There's not much time.'

'You'd better come in then,' I said with ill grace.

She went to the desk and absent-mindedly began to move my notebooks around. 'I came to tell you a secret,' she said, 'as long as you swear you won't tell anyone.'

I was irritated by her conspiratorial playfulness. 'What is it, then?' I said, sounding snappish.

Jenny took no notice of my shortness. 'I'm running away with Charlie tonight,' she said. I remember noticing she was whispering like people do in church. 'We're going to be married. It's all arranged.' She didn't seem able to take the silly, shy smile off her face. 'He's coming to pick me up from the well-house at midnight. We can stay with a friend of his who'll take us to Porterstown in the morning on his way to work, and then we'll catch the bus to Galway. It's all worked out.'

'I'm pleased for you,' I said as warmly as I could. 'It's exciting. And so romantic! How do you feel? Are you nervous?'

'You won't tell anyone, will you? Not till after we've gone. You'd probably be better off not saying anything or they may think you're in on it.'

'They'll be terribly upset,' I said.

'I wish I could see their faces when they find out tomorrow,' Jenny said. Then she hesitated, 'At least, I'd like to see Patience's face. She'll be furious. She'll be so afraid of what people will say. Serves her right. What people, anyway? She doesn't know anyone. But I'm sorry about Hilda, she'll be hurt more than angry. And she'll worry about me, not knowing what's happened.'

It seems ridiculous now that a thirty-one year old woman should be so anxious about leaving home, but then, in that house, I understood her concern. 'Write to her later, tell her you're happy.'

'I thought of that, but, you see, it's risky. There'd be a post-mark, wouldn't there? They might set the police looking for us, and Charlie isn't legal. We'll have to stay in the area, or somewhere quite near, we haven't enough money to get right away, and Carlos can only get casual work; we know that.'

'Write her a note before you go,' I said. 'Tell her how you feel. And I'll give it to her tomorrow – after you've gone. I'll say you left it in the study and I found it with my papers.'

'Would you do that? Really? She might not believe you, about finding the note. She might think you know where I've gone.'

'Well, I won't know, will I? I can't tell her what I don't know. But it'll help put her mind at rest. Here, do it now, and I'll hide it in my notebook till tomorrow.'

Jenny took the pen that I held out to her. She thought for a moment, then threw it down on the desk. 'I can't,' she said. 'I don't know what to say.'

I was impatient. Jenny seemed to be making things more difficult than they really were. 'Oh,' I said, 'just say you've met Carlos and you love him and you want to marry him. Say you're going away tonight and you're very happy and you hope she'll understand and forgive you, and tell her you love her. Just say anything, it doesn't matter. What matters is that you're telling her. That'll mean a lot to her one day, I'm sure it will. And thank her for what she's done for you. Tell her that.'

'Hey, slow down, I can't keep up,' Jenny said. She held the pen in an awkward way, almost as though she were stirring something in the kitchen. She breathed hard as she wrote. Her handwriting was big and careful, like a schoolgirl's. When she had finished, she pushed the paper towards me. 'Here,' she said. 'That's done.'

I took the letter without looking at it and put the single sheet of paper into the notebook lying open on the desk. Then I closed it. 'Don't worry about it,' I said. 'I'll make sure she gets it as soon as you and Carlos are clear away.'

Jenny hesitated at the door. 'Look,' she said, 'there's something you should know.'

I wanted her to go. 'Know what?' I asked.

'You've been kind to me,' she said. 'I owe you.'

'Don't,' I said, afraid she was going to start thanking me. 'I'm glad to help.'

But she persisted. 'Haven't you ever wondered about the Durrants? About what they've been so afraid of all these years? Don't you want to know why they all lived like hermits?'

'They don't need other people,' I said. 'Isn't that what happy families are all about?' I wasn't going to start some sort of psychological speculation with Jenny about Patience and Hilda. I wished she'd leave me alone.

'God, you're so naive,' Jenny said. 'You've spent all this time studying those old diaries and everything and you still don't even suspect.'

I didn't like being called naive, particularly by her. Probably because it was true. 'What?' I said. 'What are you trying to tell me?'

I can hear her voice now. There was no trace of the rough accent. She sounded breathless, almost as if she was afraid of the effect of what she had to say. She said, 'The great Cecil Durrant was a terrible painter and a worse philosopher. He was a bore, for God's sake, not a genius at all. The whole Cecil Durrant mystique is a chimera, and none of the Durrants can admit it.'

I couldn't take in what she was saying. 'It can't be true,' I said. 'Why are you lying to me? Wadhurst Carpenter didn't think so,' I said. 'And he should know.'

'You don't get it, do you?' Jenny said, and she wasn't sneering, she pitied me. 'Your precious Wadhurst was in love with him. He was a pervert. Didn't you ever even suspect it?'

'No,' I said, 'it's not true. You're making it up.'

'I'm not lying,' Jenny said. 'I've got a letter to prove it. While you're all at dinner I'll sneak back here and leave it for you. I'll put it with my note to Hilda. Then you'll see.'

And then she was gone, closing the door quietly behind her.

twenty-seven

That evening at Balcurran House, time crawled. I went to my room as soon as I could get away and watched the second hand on the alarm clock tick at tortoise pace, scarcely seeming to move. It was going to be hours before I dared creep down to the study to read the letter Jenny had said she'd leave there as proof of her staggering claim about Wadhurst Carpenter. I had to wait until well after everyone was asleep. It would be too awful if Patience or Hilda caught me in the study and wanted to know what the letter said. The image of Patience's heavy hand crushing the skull of that trapped mouse filled my mind and I could not get the small sharp sound of the bone cracking out of my head.

I tried to sleep, but I couldn't be still. I thought of Jenny, waiting impatiently in her own room for the early hours when she would dare to leave the house and go to meet Carlos.

In the end, I got up and stared out of the window, listening to the thudding of the waves. It wasn't late, before midnight. I leaned by forehead against the window pane to cool my pounding head. It had started to rain. It seemed always to be raining in this place.

There was a light on in one of the downstairs rooms, casting a pool of blurred light onto the garden. I moved back as the outline of a woman moved slowly across the window. Then the curtains were closed. The light came from Cecil Durrant's study. As my eyes grew accustomed to the dark, I saw a shadow come round the side of the house. Someone moved slowly across the lawn. It was Patience. Her massive silhouette was unmistakable, as was that slow gait of hers, like a statue getting under way. Then she disappeared.

Why was Patience out there in the shadows? There was something wrong. I'd sensed something in the atmosphere over dinner. The meal had been horrific. I hadn't been able to eat, and could scarcely speak, I was overwhelmed by what Jenny had told me only an hour before. The Durrants pretended not to notice my distress. They made conversation about the garden, and the indisposition of the little Pekinese. Then, when Hilda went out to get the coffee, Patience asked, 'What's wrong, dear? Is it something to do with your work?'

To fob her off, I said something vague about being distracted by something Jenny had remembered about Wadhurst Carpenter and promised to tell me. She showed no sign of particular interest, but I knew she was suddenly alert.

'Oh,' she said, in the particular way Patience has when she's dismissing something as uninteresting, 'I should be careful about believing anything Jenny has to say. She's a dear child, but she's mischievous. I don't see what she can possibly know about Wadhurst Carpenter that could interest you.'

I noticed again that her eyes had irises with definite rings of colour, like cross sections of a flint pebble, and when I looked into them I felt I was being sucked into her brain. It was spooky, as though she was putting a spell on me, and like a fool I sort of blurted out, 'She says she's got a letter to prove what she says.'

She just said 'Really?' Nothing else. Then I burst into tears. At least that stopped her asking questions. She was awfully embarrassed, and didn't know what to do and in the end she patted my cheek in a vague way.

'Take no notice of Jenny,' she said. 'I'm afraid she's got a very warped sense of humour sometimes. She doesn't mean it, but she can be very cruel.' And that was it. Hilda came in with the coffee and they talked about the garden again. Surely, there was nothing in that snatch of conversation that could so disturb Patience that she would break the habit of a lifetime and walk at night. Was it possible she could be afraid of what Jenny might be going to reveal? There was a cold, sick feeling of fear in my stomach; fear of what lengths Patience might go to in order to stop Jenny giving me her information, or me from using it.

I thought of Jenny, waiting in the dark in her room for the early hours when she could creep out and go to Carlos. I thought of the two of them, walking five miles to the village in the dark before dawn, soaked to the skin. If Jenny were a proper romantic heroine in a Gothic tale, she'd catch pneumonia and choke to death in Carlos's arms in a garret or a paupers' hospital, with Hilda and Patience pounding at the doors.

I imagined the rain dripping from the roof slates of the well-house in a melancholy rhythm like a subdued funeral march; the wet stone dull black, an evil-looking fungus growing on the half-rotted door post. Carlos could be there already, waiting for Jenny, knowing there were still hours before she could dare leave the house.

It was no good. I got up and slipped out of my room, feeling my way slowly along the wall and down the stairs. My feet felt icy as I crept across the flagged entrance hall. As silently as I could, I opened the door of Cecil Durrant's study and turned on the light.

There was a letter – or rather a page from a letter – lying on Cecil Durrant's desk beside my notebook. I recognized Wadhurst Carpenter's big, bold handwriting.

My notebook lay closed where I'd left it. I opened it to take Jenny's note to Hilda upstairs with me. But it wasn't there. There was no sign of any note where I thought I'd left it. I took the notebook by the spine to shake it. Nothing.

twenty-eight

I remembered searching everywhere I could think of for that note, but it wasn't there. Finally I picked up the page of Wadhurst Carpenter's handwriting on the desk. This was the evidence that Jenny had promised me.

I found it again among the papers strewn on my mother's bed. It was an extract from a letter written to Caroline Durrant, dated 24 February 1935:

... in conclusion, dearest Mrs D, I beg you to make any calls upon me which might make life without our best beloved any easier for you or his daughters. Anything at all. You know how I have always loved him, as I know how much you did also. He was much more to me than a father, more even than an ordinary friend; I have always imagined that we were akin to the Ancient Greek concept of brotherhood between men of action.

I have always been grateful and honoured that you once allowed a place for me in the sacred circle of the love which you and he shared. Indeed, in spite of my absence of recent years, we are bound together, you and I and he, as a loving family on a true and pure basis of love and affection. You, his wife and the mother of his children,

STRANGER IN THE HOUSE

have given me the greatest gift of all, that in no aspect of your family life did I ever feel like a stranger in your house.

I must also express to you my gratitude for keeping the secret that only you and I share. What I did was degrading and unforgivable, and you know how bitterly I regret my actions. To tell the truth, I scarcely knew what I did, I am ashamed, at my stage of life, of the degree of innocence I had in these matters. I came to the funeral as I did seeking reconciliation with you. I hoped, just once more in my lifetime, to be close to my friend of friends. I accept now that you could not forgive me for the past and so, failing in my purpose, rejected, as I saw it, by my own family, I turned to what small comfort was offered. The woman will not be a loser. Thank God your daughters, whom I love as dear sisters, have no suspicion of the truth. My issue is blessed, and I thank you from the bottom of my heart that, even after our beloved's passing, you are permitting a piece of me, and my love for your husband, to go with you into the future. I pray this may reflect for all of you my undying devotion to Cecil Durrant and his family.

I remember how I'd fled back to my bedroom at Balcurran House with that letter. There I read it and re-read it. I couldn't understand what there was in it that had led Jenny to believe what she had. I could see at once that it proved nothing. But Jenny was a crude and foolish girl. I was annoyed with her because I had believed her, or, at least, I had been prepared to believe her. Part of me had wanted to believe her, I suppose. Such a revelation would have given me a bestseller. I should have known she was a silly girl, stupid and malicious. Perhaps not malicious. Perhaps she had so little real understanding of the various nature of love to see the possibility of devotion without lewdness.

I don't know what Jenny had in mind when she told me her suspicions. Perhaps she believed what she said and wanted to tell the truth, to wipe the slate clean and explode the past as she moved on into a future with Carlos. Maybe she wanted to help me because I had helped her. Perhaps she wanted to destroy the Durrant myth for ever. But gradually the implications of the rest of the letter had dawned on me. It was suddenly clear that the child Wadhurst Carpenter mentioned must be Jenny. Only Jenny, joined to the Durrant's future by adoption, could have been 'the piece of him'.

Trying to work out what might have happened, I'd thought that Kathleen, full of hatred for the Durrants, might well have seduced Wadhurst Carpenter. Had she told Mrs Durrant who was the father of her unborn child when she'd come to the house and been hustled away to some refuge where she could have the baby? I remembered Jenny telling me about the stranger whom Molly Dunn had hidden in the well-house. That must have been Wadhurst Carpenter, come to see his daughter. And poor stupid Jenny had no idea of who her father was, even when it was there before her in that letter she couldn't see it, and it was the last thing the Durrants would tell her. When she found the letter, it would have been easy enough for her, stunned by the admission of the perversion which she thought she'd seen in it, to miss the implication of that final paragraph. I didn't think Patience and Hilda had known either. It was Mrs Durrant's secret; hers and Wadhurst Carpenter's. Caroline Durrant would not reveal such a secret.

But Patience had discovered it. She'd discovered it that night when I'd seen a woman's silhouette against the light in

Cecil Durrant's study and then watched Patience stumble away across the lawn towards the laurel walk. She had found that letter where Jenny left it, she'd managed to read it, and then, perhaps hearing Hilda coming to find her, she'd dropped it and left the room before her sister could see the shocking truth – that Jenny was the daughter of the banished, morally depraved, Wadhurst Carpenter.

twenty-nine

I was too confused to sleep that night. I was afraid without being sure what it was I feared. Balcurran House, its dark, laurel-shrouded grounds, the sound of the ruthless sea pounding the rocks, all threatened me. My bedroom light swayed in a draught from the window, making grotesque shadows on the walls. There was a sound of scratching. It didn't sound like mice. It came from the window. I thought the wind had set a branch of the wisteria rubbing against the pane. But then there was another sound, a sharp tapping this time. I got up to see what it was.

It was almost dawn. I put on a dressing-gown and opened the window, then nearly screamed as Jenny's face appeared from the tangle of leaves and boughs. 'I thought you'd never hear me,' she said. Her teeth were chattering. I pulled her over the sill and she dropped onto the floor. Her hair was wet and her face streaked with mud. She still looked like a Pre-Raphaelite Ophelia, but this time an Ophelia pulled from the dirty river.

I shut the window and pulled a blanket off the bed to wrap round her. I thought she was shivering with cold, but then I realized that she was shuddering with painful, soundless, sobbing.

'What happened?' I put the blanket close around her. She looked up at me with a bleak expression, shaking her head, tears pouring down her face. 'Did you get caught? Where's Carlos now?' Jenny let out a howl. I quickly put my hand over her mouth to stifle the sound. 'Shhh,' I warned. 'Did he get away?'

Jenny shook her head. She took a long, juddering breath. 'He wasn't there,' she said.

'He wasn't there?'

'He doesn't love me.' I could scarcely make out what she was saying because her voice was so thick with tears. 'He didn't mean it, any of it. I waited ages and he never came.'

'Perhaps something went wrong with his plans. Something must have happened and he couldn't let you know in time.'

'No, it's not that. You get a feeling. It's all over now. My life's over. I was crazy to think he could really love me.' She sniffed, then dropped the blanket from her shoulders and got up. 'I'm sorry I had to wake you. I couldn't get in. I didn't think I'd be coming back so I didn't take a key. I left my suitcase at the well-house.'

There was nothing I could say to comfort her. There was nothing to say at all. I picked up the blanket she'd let drop and folded it. 'I'll come with you to the well-house in the morning when Patience has gone to work,' I said. 'Maybe we'll find a note from Carlos explaining what happened.'

I gave myself a jolt when I said the word. A note? What about Jenny's note to Hilda? Patience must have taken it from my notebook. In spite of her failing sight, she must have seen it was addressed to Hilda. She'd have given it to her sister. They would have known about Jenny's plans to elope? They could have stopped him coming, waylaid him and told him they would call the police and have him arrested if he came on their land. Carlos's English wasn't good but he'd understand the word police.

There was no point in saying anything to Jenny now. She seemed to want to be alone and I let her go. There was nothing I could do. What could I have done? Perhaps Carlos was always playing her along. Perhaps he got scared? If I were in his shoes, I'd be scared stiff of taking on Jenny, particularly when that meant risking the wrath of the Durrants. Or more likely the revenge of the Durrants.

thirty

For years I have tried hard to forget what happened at Balcurran House the day after that dreadful night. I told myself it was something I made up, and sometimes I thought I'd succeeded, but it was still there, at the back of my memory. And sometimes, even though forty years had passed, that final day at Balcurran felt as though it could have been yesterday.

First thing in the morning, I went to Cecil Durrant's study and began a search of the desk for Jenny's note to Hilda. I looked through all my piles of loose papers and sifted through the drawers in case it had slipped down some crevice. There was no sign of it. I started again.

Then from the road I heard the sound of a car accelerating and the crash of a missed gear change. That was Hilda on her way to the village. I left off the search for the note. With Hilda out of the house, now was the best chance of bringing the suitcase back to Jenny's room unseen. I put on my coat and climbed out of the open study window to make my way to the well-house. I didn't want to risk leaving by the back door in case Patience in her office overlooking the yard should hear me and be curious as to why I was taking time off from working on my book. I didn't want her asking questions at lunch.

I can see the well-house as clearly as if I were there now. It looked forlorn and derelict in the grey morning. The grass around it had been flattened by the wind and was choked with dead leaves blown from the shrubbery. I'd have given anything not to have to go in, but I opened the creaking door. It had rained heavily in the night and there was the sound of dripping. The damp earth on the floor showed no sign of being disturbed, but the pile of folded blankets in the corner had been moved, thrown into an untidy heap under the window with the sleeping bag. There was a torch on top of them. That's where Jenny would have waited, staring out into the darkness waiting for Carlos to come. One of the blankets had been pulled out to conceal Jenny's suitcase. The sight of that suitcase made me sad. I hadn't realized how much I'd wanted Jenny to escape to a new life, which even though hard, would have been full of normal things, like work and friends and children and a home and television and going to the cinema or for a drink and … well, everything that anyone else would take for granted.

I began to pick up the blankets and fold them. The last blanket lay across the rim of the well itself. I pulled it towards me. It was wet. As I moved it, the dripping grew louder and faster. There was water leaking through the roof. It must have soaked the blanket lying across the wooden well-cover. But with the blanket gone, the drips were falling straight into the water of the well itself, that's why they seemed so loud. I could hear them echo up the shaft.

I leaned over and as I touched the wooden slats of the cover, one of them fell away and dropped down. I waited for the splash. But the impact was not with water. I looked more closely. Since I had last seen it, the rotted wood of the cover had fallen away almost entirely. I noticed what looked like claw marks on one of the remaining struts. The words of the old nursery rhyme echoed in my head ... *Ding dong bell, pussy's in the well....* It did indeed look as though some poor cat had jumped on the cover and it had given way. What a horrible death, I thought, and I shuddered at the sight of the despairing gouges in the wood.

I picked up the torch and leaned forward to shine it down the well shaft into the water. I had to make sure in case there wasn't a cat or some other animal still swimming round trying to get out. The beam of the torch made its way across the sleek black surface of the water. The light flickered, then came to rest on an upturned human face. I almost dropped the torch. 'Carlos!' I said aloud.

In my mind's eye now, I can see his eyes staring at me out of that ghastly rubbery mask of his face. He was young, a boy; previously I'd taken him to be older, but he was only a boy. It took me years before I stopped seeing him in my dreams at night.

At the time I just felt blind panic. There was no question of stopping to think.

I fled.

I fled from the well-house and across the stretch of grass towards the shrubbery. I crashed into the shelter of the laurels and rhododendrons until their tangled boughs brought me to a halt. I was gasping for breath. I could not rid myself of the sight of wide white eyes staring from the huge dark face in the flickering torchlight. I didn't think what I was doing. I felt compelled to get as far away from the well-house as I could. If anyone had appeared and tried to stop me, I knew I would have brushed them aside, knocked them down, even, so overwhelming was my need to escape.

Panic drove me on, but my legs were heavy and my lungs felt sore. I came up against a tree and clung to its trunk. I tried to tell myself to get a grip, but I was still in a panic. The dark and forbidding house was ahead of me, and the open window of Cecil Durrant's study. I jumped for the sill and pulled myself over. I landed awkwardly, but on my feet. For a moment I held my breath and waited, listening to make sure that no one had heard me.

My handbag was on the desk. I had to have my handbag. It held my cheque book. There was no time for anything else. My notes, clothes, a scrawl to explain my disappearance, there was time for none of those things. I had to get away.

Then I saw Patience. She was sitting in Cecil Durrant's chair, staring through me out of the open window. Her face was like granite, expressionless. It was too late for me to go back. I could hear the blood thumping in my head. I couldn't understand how she didn't hear it too. But she still stared at me with her stony eyes without any sign that she knew I was there.

I tried to pull myself together. My handbag was close to her right hand. I had to have my handbag. She's blind, I told myself. She can't see you. Be quiet and she won't know you're here. I crept forward. Behind me in the garden the bamboos rustled. Patience did not move. I kept my eyes fixed on the handbag.

I reached the desk and stealthily put out my hand to grab it. Then my wrist was caught in an ice-cold grip and I was pulled forward across the desktop. Patience pushed her face at me, her teeth bared in fury. Her eyes burned into mine. Oh, God, I thought, she's mad.

She snarled at me. 'You've betrayed us. All this time you

were deceiving us.' She still had her vice-like grip clamped on my wrist. The pain was unbearable, but I couldn't catch my breath to scream.

'No,' I managed to groan, 'no.'

'Then what are these?' she hissed. Sheets of paper covered in my handwriting lay scattered over the top of the desk. In front of her lay pages and pages in my handwriting. They were the letters I had sent to Alison.

The Durrant sisters had never posted them. They'd read what I'd written about them. They could never forgive that betrayal of their trust. I looked at Patience's face and I was terror-struck. Her face was contorted with hatred. 'You recognize them, don't you? Your letters to your friend in England and all the things you've written about us. You came here to destroy us. You came to make out my father was a liar and a cheat. You wormed your way into our home with lies about admiring him and you betrayed us.'

I shook my head, trying to get her to release her grip. 'No,' I said again. My voice sounded feeble, terrified.

She stood up and jerked me forward so that the edge of the desk rammed into my ribs. For a moment I was winded. 'You mock him,' she screamed at me. 'Do you deny that?'

'It wasn't like that,' I muttered. My head was swimming with pain.

'A hypocrite! You'd make him out to be a hypocrite.' Her chilling eyes glared at me. How could I ever have thought that she was blind?

'You have betrayed us and you will pay,' she said, her voice suddenly cold. I had a vision of that little mouse skull popping under that giant fist. I cringed away from her.

'Listen to me.' I was pleading with her. How could I explain? 'Let me go,' I said.

Suddenly she was calm. Her eyes went blank again. For a moment, drawn into their flint-like vortex, I had a glimpse of the depth of misery she had buried behind the detached stare of an unseeing Sphinx.

'You know you can't go now,' she said. 'I can't let you go. You cannot leave here with the knowledge that you have. You must stay here.'

'You've got it wrong,' I said. 'What I know could never harm you. I would never do that.'

'You don't know what you're talking about,' she said. 'Destroy our father and you destroy us all. We can never trust you.'

'You can't keep me here,' I said. 'My parents know I'm here.'

She smiled then. It was the kindly smile of an old, wise, ordinary woman. 'I don't think your parents would be too surprised if you took off to America or accepted a job in Africa at a moment's notice, do you, my dear. From what I've seen and heard while you've been here, I don't think you're very close to them, are you? You see, Frances, I was right not to trust you. You are deceitful by nature.'

For a fleeting moment, the eyes came back to life. She looked full at me as though she could see inside my head. 'Cheat,' she said. 'Liar.' She put her head back and spat at me and for a moment she relaxed her grip on my arm.

I tore my wrist out of her grasp, grabbed my handbag and leaped for the windowsill to escape.

I heard her behind me, but she was slow. I was out of the window before she could catch hold of me, and once outside I ran around the side of the house and towards the main gate as though the demons of hell were after me. I could hear her voice behind me, mocking me. 'You'll never escape,' she cried. 'Run, but you won't get free.'

I had taken the long way to the main gate, but if I went through the courtyard onto the cliff road, Jenny might see me. I couldn't face Jenny. How could I tell Jenny about her Spanish boy?

As I staggered on, my feet slipping on the wet grass, trying to hurry but scarcely making progress across the rough ground, I felt that the house itself was trying to prevent my escape. It seemed to me that everyone in that benighted place was damned. Nothing good could ever happen there. The Durrants were crazed, Patience as well as Hilda. They were all mad. Perhaps Jenny already knew about Carlos, perhaps she did it. Then I told myself, Jenny loved him. But that could have been a motive, if he had turned up last night and told her he wouldn't go with her. She could have lost her temper and struggled with him and he went into the well. But then I remembered how distraught she'd been in my bedroom when she thought he hadn't come for her. That sobbing woman didn't kill him. But someone did, and if it wasn't Jenny, who was it? I couldn't believe it had been an accident, not when he knew the state of the well-cover better than anyone. He'd spent enough time alone there, he must have known.

I was almost to the main gates. I could see the wrought iron bars through the rhododendrons. The gates were locked, of course, but I could climb out over the fence, the way I had climbed in on the night when I first arrived.

My head was swimming. I concentrated on climbing the fence and dropped down onto the roadside. I began to walk back the way I thought the taxi had brought me that first night. I was not sure I had chosen the right direction. I mustn't go near the village. Hilda would be there. I walked on, constantly imagining that I was hearing a car on the road, a car that could be Hilda's.

I was sure then that Hilda had killed Carlos. Hilda had seen Jenny's note, Patience had given it to her. Patience was on the lawn last night, trying to come to terms with the knowledge that Wadhurst Carpenter was Jenny's father. She must have met Hilda returning with the dogs and given her Jenny's note. Hilda would go to any lengths to stop Jenny from going away with Carlos. Perhaps she saw Jenny bringing shame on the name of Durrant with an unsuitable marriage; perhaps she wanted to protect Jenny from something she thought would make her unhappy; perhaps long-ago sexual frustration boiled over in a frenzy of jealousy: Whatever her motives, Hilda set out to prevent the elopement. Maybe she'd intended only to send Carlos away, pay him off, perhaps, or threaten him. But it had gone wrong.

I imagined how it must have been. Poor Carlos would have been at the well-house. When he heard Hilda coming, he'd have thought it was Jenny. He would have been off his guard. But Hilda knew he was there. She knew the well-house was a hiding place. She was ready. Perhaps she knocked him over the head with something, perhaps she simply pushed him and, off-balance, he fell through the well-cover. After all, I told myself, Hilda had killed this way before. I was sure that she'd killed Kathleen, Jenny's mother. Probably she had, I corrected myself. Possibly.

I visualized Hilda, with her jerky movements and her long pointy nose, always vague and flurried, with her fussy sweetness and her darling little doggies and her poor little birdies; Hilda, so soft-hearted she couldn't kill a fly, the last person on earth who'd ever murder anybody or anything.

Hilda who had held a woman captive in the well-house and starved her almost to death. And I thought of Patience killing the mouse with one chop of her hand, the poor creature's little skull cracking with a small, sharp sound. And Patience had wanted to kill me, there was no mistaking the murder in her eyes.

The road took a sudden turn and I found myself walking on a cliff top overlooking a rocky stretch of coast. Rain clouds gripped the horizon in an iron fist. The sea, even on this still day, sucked and spat at the rockface far below. Further out to sea, beyond the outcrops of black rock, the water eddied and swirled in boiling patterns. The road seemed to cling to the cliff, holding on for its life.

I thought I heard the sound of a car's gears crashing behind me. I stopped and listened for an engine. It was hard to tell over the sound of the sea. If it was Hilda, I was done for, there was nowhere to hide. There was another crashing gear change and a small van appeared round the corner, labouring up the hill. I ran out into the road and it stopped. It was driven by an old man with a shapeless hat pulled down across his forehead. Not the quickest getaway car, but better than nothing.

I made polite conversation with the old man as he drove me towards somewhere he said I could pick up a bus that would start me on my journey to Dublin. The windscreen wipers counted off the metres as we left Balcurran House further behind. All the time I was willing him to go faster, to get further away from that house. He was a good old man. He didn't ask questions. And then the sound of the wheels of the bus to Galway City on the long stretches of empty road hummed a refrain in my head, one more mile, one more mile. Then later in the train to Dublin, the sound changed: 'I've got away,' it repeated, 'I've got away. I'm free.'

It was half-way across the Irish Sea on the plane to London that my sense of relief began to turn to doubt. I couldn't believe what I had done. All my work left behind, all the clothes I had brought with me to cold, damp Ireland, the winter clothes I was going to need more than ever now in November Newcastle. I stared out of the aircraft window at an endless vista of grey-blue sky above, grey-blue sea below. All my work, the notes I'd made, the references, the evidence for everything which might convince a publisher there was a market for a book on Wadhurst Carpenter, all left behind and now impossible to recover. To hell with the clothes, they didn't really matter, but I had to get my notes. Perhaps Jenny would send them. And then the idea occurred to me that the Durrants would probably think I'd fallen off a cliff or been murdered or something awful like that, the police were probably doing a full-scale search at that very moment, and the coastguards and air-sea rescue helicopters and tracker dogs.... Oh, my God ... when they didn't find me, or rather my body, they'd think I'd been swept away.

In the days after I arrived back in Newcastle, I tried not to think about the Durrants. I couldn't tell my parents. Not about Carlos, not about Hilda and Patience. They thought I'd simply finished my research. They talked cheerfully about my book on Wadhurst Carpenter. I'd told them some cock and bull story about my suitcase coming on by sea to explain why I returned home freezing cold without an overcoat and carrying only a handbag.

It had taken me ages, weeks, anyway, to decide to write to Jenny. Then one morning when both my parents were out, I sat at the dining room table downstairs with pen and paper looking for the right words, for any words at all.

Several times I started to explain what I'd done, then tore up what I'd written. There was nothing I could say. In the end I wrote a brief note asking her to send on the notebooks I'd left behind in Cecil Durrant's study. As for my clothes, Jenny could have anything that was any use to her.

I folded the letter and addressed an envelope. I hoped Jenny would get it before the Durrants saw it. It was the best I could do. And then I unfolded it and added a postscript. It was as though I couldn't stop myself. I wrote fast, the words tumbling out onto the paper.

You should know that the morning when I went to the well-house to get your suitcase I saw Carlos's body in the well. There was no doubt he was dead. I had the idea that Hilda found out that you were going away with him and killed him. I think you should know what happened to him, if you don't already. He did love you enough to come to meet you that night, Jenny, he wanted to marry you and then he was killed.

I did not read through what I had written. I went straight out to post it before I could have second thoughts. Or any thoughts at all.

I could never tell anyone, not Jenny, nor Alison, nor, later, my kind, understanding husband, about the thought that above all I tried to forget, the one that still wakes me in the night so that I start up in a sweat and am afraid to go back to sleep.

It was all my fault. Everything that happened was my

fault. It was I, in going there, who'd brought the real world to Balcurran House and, in doing so, destroyed their time-warp existence.

thirty-one

The letters I wrote to Alison lay strewn over my mother's bed. Forty years ago, Hilda stole my letters and read them to Patience. Those comic scenes I'd written to Alison had sealed my fate, they were a death sentence.

The letters were now spread across the bedspread in front of me. The pages covered in the excited rushed scrawl which was the handwriting of my younger self seemed to have nothing to do with me now. Letters are not like photographs, I can't look at them to see how time has changed the physical person I was then. In my head, in everything I do and feel, my past happened to another person.

They were returned to me in a big brown envelope in the post one morning about a month or six weeks after I got home. The envelope had an Irish stamp but no postmark that I could read. I found it hard to bear the thought of Hilda and Patience checking on what I was saying about them. And then there was the rest of it. In the envelope with the letters was a handful of pages torn from Cecil Durrant's diaries, and a newspaper cutting; no note, nothing else. Not a sign of who had sent it. The clipping was a page from a Galway newspaper dated two weeks before. The main story was marked with a black cross.

It fell out when I shook the envelope. I picked it up. Over the years I'd managed to block this out, but I had to face it one day. I started to read it, remembering how I'd felt the first time.

'Tragic Sisters Die in Suicide Pact?' ran the headline.

'Gardí officers from Galway have been called in to investigate the deaths of the Durrant sisters, Patience (64) and Hilda (62) of Balcurran House. The bodies of the women were discovered together in a sitting room after firemen were called to their isolated home on the Connemara coast. The fire was started in the kitchen and swept through much of the house. Firemen suspect arson.

The Gardí are working on the theory that Hilda Durrant stabbed her sister to death in a bizarre suicide pact, then started the fire herself and took poison. At first it was thought that the sisters, who were known locally as 'The Hermits on the Hill' may have been unable to cope any longer and decided to end it all. But after further forensic tests and autopsy reports, the Gardí now suspect foul play and want to question itinerant Spanish hotel worker Carlos Fernandez Garcia, who has been living rough in the area and has not been seen since he sought work at Balcurran House.

Patience and Hilda Durrant were the daughters of the distinguished explorer and religious painter Cecil Durrant, who died in 1935. The sisters had lived for many years as recluses, but earlier in life both had been well-known in their own chosen fields. Patience Durrant was a plant geneticist of note, while Hilda's detailed paintings of flowers and insects were once much in demand in scientific publications.

Yesterday, Miss Jenny Durrant, the sisters' adopted daughter and sole heir, told Inspector Brian Fogarty, who is heading the Gardí investigation, that she had seen an itinerant of Spanish appearance calling himself Carlos in the vicinity of Balcurran House. She said that on the day of the tragedy she had left the house after lunch to walk the five miles to Porterstown to post important letters. By the time she returned, firemen had put out the blaze and found the bodies.

The fire service and police were called after Joe Phelan, skipper of the trawler *Pride of Galway*, who was fishing off-shore at the time, spotted the flames at sea and alerted the coastguard on the ship's radio. Miss Jenny Durrant said the deceased had been in good spirits when she last saw them, though she knew that they were worried about their failing health.

Miss Durrant told this newspaper that as the only surviving member of the family she intends to create a Durrant memorial on the site.

'I intend to preserve it as a fitting celebration of the Durrant family,' she said. 'I have no intention of leaving. Balcurran House is my home, I belong here. My family roots are there.'

Balcurran House had been the Durrant family home since Cecil Durrant moved there to paint his greatest work, a series of huge masterpieces in oils based on his pilgrimages in foreign lands entitled *The Making Of The English Church: The Flowering of Christianity*.

That was all. I felt as I did that day in January or February 1967 when I first read the cutting. My mouth was dry, my heart beating very fast, the blood thumping in my head. I took a closer look at the newspaper cutting itself. The story filled most of the page. There was also a blur of dark grey which was apparently an aerial photograph of the smouldering ruins of Balcurran House.

I thought I understood. This was Jenny's reply to my letter. She'd read what I said about Carlos, and she'd gone to the well-house and she'd found him. She knew for sure then, if she'd had any real doubts, that Carlos had come to meet her, that he wanted to be with her, that they'd been going to be happy, she knew he wouldn't kill himself. She wouldn't think it an accident. And I'd pointed the finger at Hilda. I'd said I'd suspected her. She'd believed me. It didn't matter who'd actually pushed the Spanish boy to his death. As far as Jenny was concerned, the Durrants had killed him simply by being who and what they were. So she had killed all that remained of the family blood, because of what they'd done to her. And she had burned Balcurran, the house that symbolized everything the family stood for. Carlos was a convenient suspect.

I gathered the scattered papers together to put back in the box. I would throw it all away.

thirty-two

In the summer of 2005, I spent some weeks lecturing at Trinity College, Dublin. I had a few days free before returning to London to read the proofs of my new book, a comparative study of urban and rural social conditions at the start of the First World War.

I told myself I wanted to see something of Ireland; that's why I was driving a hire car west – Athlone, Athenry, Oughterard and on towards the coast, on, indeed, to Balcurran House. I had to lay those old ghosts to rest. I had to go back to see the place one more time.

The car climbed the cliff road and on a warm, quiet day I had the windows open and could hear the waves breaking on the rocks below the cliffs. It was very different from the cataclysmic crashing of the sea against the cliffs that I remembered here. Could it have been always stormy weather in 1966?

Everything around me seemed on a much smaller scale than the way I remembered it. Then I saw the wrought iron gates between the vast stone posts at the entrance to what was the overgrown drive to Balcurran House; the peeling painted board on the gatepost still read BALCURRAN HOUSE ONLY. TRESPASSERS WILL BE PROSECUTED. It was all just as shabby and the chain and padlock on the gates looked as though it hadn't been unlocked since I was last here.

I got out of the car and stood for a moment looking through the wrought iron bars. I was trying to recapture some of the terror with which this place once filled me. But what I felt now was not fear but a sense of desolation at what I had lost of my former self over the long years.

The wooden stile to the right of the gates had rotted away, but there was still a gap which looked as though it had become the beat of badgers or foxes. On an impulse, I clambered through. There were still brambles creeping across the drive. The path was more shadowed now as the laurels had grown across and shut out the light.

I came to the place where I remembered having my first sight of Balcurran House in the moonlight, looming from the dense shrubbery, a vast red brick building with glaring windows reflecting bright cloud – threatening and impassive.

And there it was. The battery of windows reflecting the clouds, the tangle of wisteria clambering over the pale stone of the porch, the flight of steps to the massive front door which I knew from memory looked like bones by moonlight. I had steeled myself to see a blackened ruin. It shocked me to see the place unchanged, as though nothing of the terrors that have haunted my whole life had ever happened. Jenny had been true to the promise she'd made in the newspaper after the fire. She'd said she intended to preserve Balcurran House as a fitting celebration of the Durrants, and that she had done in every detail.

Then a pack of dogs raced round the side of the house where I knew Cecil Durrant's study window would still look out on the clattering thicket of bamboos. They were a motley pack, some missing legs, ears, tails. And lumbering painfully behind them a tall, stooping woman with her bobbed greyish hair held by a schoolgirl slide. I felt all the old fear then like ice freezing the blood in my body. The years fell away and I was staring at Hilda Durrant.

I couldn't believe my eyes. For a moment, I thought I was seeing her ghost, still carrying out the same relentless routine as she did every night and had since I last saw her forty years ago. Then I realized with a kind of shock that of course it wasn't Hilda I was seeing walking the Durrant dogs. It was Jenny. Hadn't she said, standing among the ruins, 'I belong at Balcurran House. My family roots are here.'

Patience and Hilda, and their mother, too, had done their work too well. They had created her in their own image as one of them: nothing would take the Durrant out of Jenny now.

I turned before she could look back and see me and went back to the car.

I drove away from Balcurran House for ever. I remembered that when Hilda Durrant had originally agreed to let me come there, it was on the understanding that I would redress the balance of history and restore her father to his rightful place as Wadhurst Carpenter's mentor. Cecil Durrant's daughters were resentful that the pupil had expunged the master. It consoled me as I drove away to think that there was also a sneaky victory for Wadhurst Carpenter over the family which ultimately betrayed his devotion to them. Now Wadhurst Carpenter's daughter was their sole heir, curator of the Durrant name and reputation.

I suddenly felt happier than I had felt for years. At last, the Durrants had set me free.